T0001754

the
further
adventures of

SHERLOCK HOLMES

REVENGE FROM THE GRAVE

AVAILABLE NOW FROM TITAN BOOKS
THE FURTHER ADVENTURES OF SHERLOCK HOLMES SERIES:

THE GRIMSWELL CURSE
Sam Siciliano

THE DEVIL'S PROMISE
David Stuart Davies

THE ALBINO'S TREASURE
Stuart Douglas

MURDER AT SORROW'S CROWN
Steven Savile & Robert Greenberger

THE WHITE WORM
Sam Siciliano

THE RIPPER LEGACY
David Stuart Davies

THE COUNTERFEIT DETECTIVE
Stuart Douglas

THE MOONSTONE'S CURSE
Sam Siciliano

THE HAUNTING OF TORRE ABBEY
Carole Buggé

THE IMPROBABLE PRISONER
Stuart Douglas

THE DEVIL AND THE FOUR
Sam Siciliano

THE INSTRUMENT OF DEATH
David Stuart Davies

THE MARTIAN MENACE
Eric Brown

THE CRUSADER'S CURSE
Stuart Douglas

THE VENERABLE TIGER
Sam Siciliano

THE GREAT WAR
Simon Guerrier

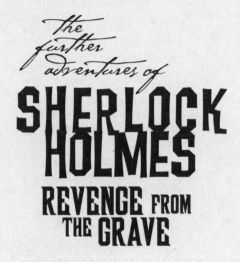

the further adventures of
SHERLOCK HOLMES
REVENGE FROM THE GRAVE

DAVID STUART DAVIES

TITAN BOOKS

THE FURTHER ADVENTURES OF SHERLOCK HOLMES:
REVENGE FROM THE GRAVE
Print edition ISBN: 9781789097924
E-book edition ISBN: 9781789097931

Published by Titan Books
A division of Titan Publishing Group Ltd
144 Southwark Street, London SE1 0UP
www.titanbooks.com

First edition: January 2022
10 9 8 7 6 5 4 3 2 1

This is a work of fiction. All of the characters, organizations, and events
portrayed in this novel are either products of the author's imagination or are
used fictitiously. Any resemblance to actual persons, living or dead (except for
satirical purposes), is entirely coincidental.

© David Stuart Davies 2022. All Rights Reserved.

David Stuart Davies asserts the moral right to be identified as the
author of this work.

No part of this publication may be reproduced, stored in a retrieval system,
or transmitted, in any form or by any means without the prior written
permission of the publisher, nor be otherwise circulated in any form of
binding or cover other than that in which it is published and without a
similar condition being imposed on the subsequent purchaser.

A CIP catalogue record for this title is available from the British Library.

Printed and bound in Great Britain by CPI Group (UK) Ltd, Croydon, CR0
4YY.

To Steven T. Doyle and Charles Prepolec

Two of my favourite American Sherlockian scholars
and dear friends

Prologue

France, January 1891

Monseigneur Charles Aubert drew back the curtains to the large French windows in his study and looked out across the moonlit gardens of the château, the shadows forming interesting patterns across the smooth surfaces of the extensive lawns. He consulted his watch. It was one minute after midnight. The she-devil was late. No doubt a ploy on her part to unsettle him.

With a sigh of irritation, he returned to his desk and withdrew a leather bag from the top drawer and fondled it, the coins within chinking gently as he did so. Placing the bag on his desk, he poured himself a glass of wine, checked the time once more and grimaced. It was then that the thought struck him that perhaps the creature would not come after all. This notion caused his heart to beat faster. He had to have those letters. They must be destroyed, otherwise his life would be ruined. With some agitation he returned to the window and gazed out once more. All remained still and silent.

Where the hell was she? He had capitulated to all her demands. Offered her the ridiculous price for the letters... This blasted woman who called herself Defarge.

Suddenly, he heard a noise behind him. He turned abruptly and, staring into the shadows at the far side of the room beyond the orange flickering flames of the fireplace, he glimpsed a figure.

'You,' he croaked.

'Good evening, Monseigneur Aubert,' came the reply, as the figure moved forward into the dim light. 'You were expecting me.'

The young woman was dressed in a long cloak with a hood so that only her pale features were visible. But there was no doubt that this was his blackmailer, Madame Defarge. She seemed to have materialised out of thin air.

'You have the letters?' he barked, snatching up the leather pouch.

She smiled. 'Will you not offer your guest a drink?'

'Let us conclude this business. I have no wish to prolong matters any more than is necessary. This is not a social occasion.' Now that the fiend had put in an appearance, Aubert grew in confidence. It was clear to him that she was ready to finalise the bargain. He was not prepared to put up with her sarcastic prevarications. He thrust his hand out. 'The correspondence, please.'

Her smile broadened. 'My fee, please,' she responded.

Aubert snatched up the leather pouch and, untying the fastening, tipped the gold coins out on to the desk. They glinted in the candlelight. 'There's your blasted blood money. Now hand over the letters.'

Madame Defarge withdrew a packet from the folds of her cloak and dropped it to the floor. Without a moment's hesitation Aubert rushed forward and bent down to retrieve it. As he did so, the woman, with a swift practised movement, slipped behind him and, producing a vicious and slender dagger, slit Aubert's throat. Blood gushed and sprayed the package with a dark crimson sheen. Aubert gurgled, eyes wide with terror and shock. He managed to crawl a few yards on his hands and knees before slumping forward, the darkness of death overpowering him. She smiled with satisfaction. His removal was essential, for she knew that he would not let the matter lie. Aubert would compromise her, hound her, seek her out for revenge. With his death the trail ended here.

Madame Defarge stood for some moments staring down at her bloody conquest before picking up the packet of letters and dropping it into the fire where the eager flames quickly consumed it. She scooped up the gold coins from the desk and made an exit through the French windows.

On her return journey to Paris in her private carriage, Madame Defarge contemplated her future, one she had been considering for some months. Now she was ready to implement her plans. For a few years, using the pseudonym of Madame Defarge, courtesy of Mr Charles Dickens, she had built up a small but efficient criminal network which operated in Paris. As leader she had organised a series of daring robberies and blackmail scenarios, with the odd financially beneficial murder on the side. But now it was time for a change. France was getting too hot for her. She sensed the authorities were close on her heels. Now it was time to spread her dark wings. Now it was time to return to England.

Part One

Prelude

Chapter One

From the journal of John H. Watson, May 1894

The emotional blow I experienced following the death of Sherlock Holmes after his encounter with Professor Moriarty at the Reichenbach Falls was consolidated some six months later by the death of my wife, Mary. The loss of these two major figures from my personal landscape devastated me. For some time, the world darkened and I felt adrift from life and society. I began living a lonely pointless existence with, I am afraid to say, too much reliance on alcohol. It was only a surprise encounter with Stamford, my old friend from my days at Bart's, that helped to drag me back to the straight and narrow. It would be true to say that he ordered rather than advised me to return to general practice. 'Helping other poor souls recover their health and normality will soon help to ease your own traumas,' he said with some force. 'You are a doctor, Watson, and a good one; you should use your skills for the sake of your fellow man. Moping in bars at lunchtime is no way to exist.'

I mulled over Stamford's words and through the haze of self-pity, I saw that he was right. And so, I set about what I thought of whimsically as the 'Resuscitation of John Watson'. I set up a small medical practice in Kensington and gradually I had a comfortable patient base to set me on an even keel financially. While I could not claim to be completely happy, I did feel I had returned to humanity and was doing my best to help others and be respected for my endeavours.

True happiness came about when a strange visitor, claiming to be a decrepit old book collector, entered my consulting room on a May evening in 1894. Pulling off his false whiskers and false nose, he revealed himself as Sherlock Holmes.

My friend had returned from the dead, although, as he assured me, he had never actually died. He described to me in detail his encounter with Moriarty at the Falls and his remarkable escape. He had rid the world of the foremost criminal of the age and took advantage of the opportunity to disappear himself.

'If the world were convinced that I was dead, that I too had perished with the Professor in that cauldron of foam, it would remove my shackles – I could take a rest from crime. I could travel around the world without the burden of responsibility which I had given myself: Mr Sherlock Holmes, consulting detective. I wanted not to be consulted, for a time at least. I wished to follow my own desires, to fill my mind with other things, refresh my jaded intellect – to absent myself from the bleat of the distressed client. So rapidly does the brain work in moments of heightened tension that I had resolved to disappear – to die for a while, if you like – almost before Moriarty's body had reached the bottom of the abyss.'

I was hurt that he had not confided in me and accepted his apology for causing me the pain of believing him dead for three years. 'Always I feared your affectionate regard for me might tempt you to some indiscretion. I simply could not risk it,' he had explained.

I sighed heavily. 'You were probably right. But, Holmes, why now? What has prompted this sudden reappearance?'

My friend pursed his lips. 'To be honest, I was feeling that it was time for me to return to detective work. However, while I was contemplating this course of action, I received a communication from brother Mycroft expressing concerns about the growing criminal activity in London. He sensed that there was an organisation similar to that of Professor Moriarty on the rise again. That simple statement was enough to convince me that now was time to return to Baker Street. I packed my bags and came over at once to London. So it was that I was soon sitting in my old, battered armchair in my old rooms wishing that I could have my old friend Watson in the other chair opposite which he had so often adorned.'

My heart swelled at this observation. 'It is my dearest wish, old fellow.'

Holmes beamed. 'So it shall be. We'll have you moved in swiftly – but something else must happen first.'

'What is that?'

'To capture that marksman who had accompanied the Professor on that fateful Swiss sojourn. Now, I suggest we get some victuals down us before the rigours of the evening. What do you say to supper at Marcini's?'

In less than an hour we were seated at a discreet table in Marcini's restaurant. The old place had not changed at all from the days when Holmes and I were regulars there. Even, the head waiter, Gyles, was still in situ and greeted us like old friends. We both settled for sea bass with new potatoes and a salad, accompanied by a bottle of Montrachet. We ate mostly in silence, both savouring the quiet intimacy of our reunion dinner, but when the cigars and brandies were being consumed, I could contain my curiosity no longer.

'Tell me Holmes, what on earth have you been doing these last three years?'

My friend gazed at me with a serious expression for some moments before replying. 'I stretched and grew,' he said simply. 'I travelled to Tibet. I visited Lhassa and spent some time with the Dalai Lama. Confronting a man of such refined wisdom is intoxicating. The head spins, the spirit soars, ghosts are exorcised and the mind expands. The worn-out timbers of my brain were renewed and polished to a radiant sheen after a mere week in his company.

'Then I passed through Persia, looked in at Mecca and paid a short but interesting visit to the Khalifa at Khartoum. I even spent some months researching coal tar derivatives in Montpellier in the South of France. I had a marvellous time, although, as I intimated previously, I was acutely conscious that in my joy and mental rebirth, I had left you mourning a friend who was not dead.' He paused a moment and sighed heavily before continuing. 'And then I read of the passing of your wife – a real death this time. I reasoned that a letter of condolence from me would hardly be appropriate.' He gave me a bleak smile. 'I received a communication from Mycroft expressing his concern about the rise in crime in the city, which was the final prompt I needed to ensure my return.'

I listened with fascination to Holmes' recital, which he delivered with consummate ease. 'But tell me, why disguise yourself as a bookseller?'

'Ah, this was prompted by my investigations earlier today. At the present, I cannot go snooping around dressed as myself – I would be far too easy a target. Once I had carried out my enquiries in this persona to my satisfaction – about which I will tell you later – I decided to surprise you in your study. You know I cannot resist a touch of the dramatic.'

'And nearly gave me a heart attack.'

'Sometimes I do overstep the mark.'

'In this instance I forgive you. I cannot tell you how happy I am to see you again.'

'The feeling is mutual, old fellow.'

It was that night that we entered 'The Empty House', as I referred to the affair in my written account of the evening's dramatic events and, with the assistance of Inspector Lestrade, apprehended Colonel Sebastian Moran. It was my first encounter with this remarkable villain, but it was fated that it would not be the last.

It was after midnight when we found ourselves back in the sitting room of 221B Baker Street, satisfied with the knowledge that Moran was in the care of Scotland Yard. Our old chambers had indeed been left unchanged, through the supervision of his brother Mycroft and the immediate care of Mrs Hudson. As I entered, I saw, it is true, an unwonted tidiness, but the old landmarks were all in their place. There were the chemical corner and the acid-stained, deal-topped table. There upon a shelf was the row of formidable scrapbooks and books of reference which many of our nefarious fellow-citizens would have been so glad to burn. The diagrams, the violin-case, and the pipe rack – even the Persian slipper which contained the tobacco – all met my eyes as I glanced around me.

'And now, Watson,' said Holmes, shrugging off his outer coat, 'let me see you in your old seat once more.'

I was glad to acquiesce to my friend's request. He took his chair opposite me and we sat in companionable silence for some time. It pleased me greatly as I observed my friend's lean features in the firelight to realise that once again Mr. Sherlock Holmes was back in Baker Street and was free to devote his life to examining those interesting little problems which the complex life of London so plentifully presents.

I moved back into my old Baker Street quarters within twenty-four hours of our adventure in the empty house and it was at breakfast time the following day that we had a visit from Inspector Lestrade. He burst into our sitting room as though the very devil was on his tail. His face was flushed and his eyes were wild and troubled. Without ceremony he loured over our breakfast table and announced. 'He's gone, Mr Holmes. Slipped through our grasp.'

'Moran?' cried Holmes, half rising from his chair.

'Yes.'

'But how?'

Lestrade paused to mop his brow before replying. 'He was kept in a cell at the Yard and yesterday evening some Inspector, a fellow calling himself Pearson, turned up with documents and two constables to escort him away to Wandsworth Prison to await trial. The sergeant on duty was completely taken in by these imposters and their fake documents. So convincing were they that he passed Moran into their custody. The blighter is free again.'

Holmes banged his fist on the table in frustration. 'It is my fault. I should have warned you that his confederates may make an attempt to rescue him, though I assumed...' My friend shot an accusatory stare at the unfortunate policeman, who had the grace to look crestfallen.

'And that's not all, Mr Holmes. This Inspector Pearson left an envelope to be passed on to you.'

'To me?'

'"To Mr Sherlock Holmes Esq", it says.' Lestrade withdrew the envelope from his pocket and passed it to my friend. Holmes took it and extracted a sheet of paper from within. In reading the contents, his eyes widened and his mouth gaped in shock.

'What is it, Holmes?' I asked.

Without a word, he passed the message to me. It was written on stiff, expensive cream paper with firm angular writing in black ink. A tingle of fear ran up my spine as I read the words written there:

Just to let you know, Mr Holmes, that I have returned and I am ready to exact my revenge. Take care. Take very great care. Yours sincerely, Professor James Moriarty.'

Part Two

❧

The Game Begins

Chapter Two

From the journal of John H. Watson

Within an hour of receiving the note, Holmes had retired to his room, emerging some time later having donned a disguise as a street beggar, with a suitably grey and grubby visage. As he made his way to the door, he waved and wished me good morning before exiting without any explanation. It was early evening when he returned. Without stripping his disguise, he dropped down into his chair by the fire with a heavy sigh. 'Would you be so kind, Watson, as to pour me a brandy and soda.'

'Certainly, Holmes. You look all in.'

'A little weary, at least.'

'Was your mission successful?'

'In a way. I learned what I wanted to know – but it was information I did not particularly want to hear.'

'You are talking in riddles,' I said, handing him his drink.

'I am sorry, my dear fellow. I will explain. While I cannot believe that my old adversary is still alive – that note was no doubt an attempt to disconcert me now that I have returned to detective work – I needed to satisfy any niggling uncertainties that the message prompted. The intelligence that Mycroft passed on to me regarding the increase in organised crime in the city and the clever escape of Moran now leads me to believe that perhaps there is a remnant group of the old Moriarty gang still in operation. I set out today to find out what I could. That meant visiting Soapy Sanders.'

It was a name I had not heard before. My puzzled expression no doubt indicated as much.

'He's an old lag,' explained my friend. 'Quite a successful burglar in his day. Retired now. Age and rheumatism put paid to his larcenous endeavours. I first encountered him when I began operating as a detective – before your time. I have helped him on a few occasions to escape the clutches of the law when he has been wrongly accused. Despite his nefarious activities, he is an affable fellow with a keen nose for what is going on in the criminal underworld. He has provided me with some particularly useful information in the past – information that could not be dragged out of him by a Scotland Yarder even if they used hot irons to persuade him, but he is always happy to chat with me. The last time I saw him he was living in Shoreditch, so that is where I headed today. I soon discovered that he is no longer in residence at his old address, a decrepit slum dwelling off Blanchard Road. So, I had to begin the weary trudge around all the ale houses and gin shops in the area in search of him. I made enquiries at all the venues he used to frequent but people down that way are very suspicious of questions, even from a raddled old beggar like me.' Holmes threw out an arm to indicate his tattered and dusty ensemble.

'Well, to cut to the chase, I did find Soapy eventually, huddled in a dark corner of a grubby drinking den. The man is now a mere skeleton in rags. I fear he is not long for this life. He certainly brightened up on seeing me – when I convinced him who I really was.' Holmes chuckled at this notion. 'I bought him a glass of ale and a mutton pie which he consumed with relish. I am pleased to say that despite his poor condition, he still keeps his ear to the ground and his misty eyes open.'

'What was he able to tell you?' I asked, eager to hear the news.

'Rumours rather than facts, I am afraid, Watson, but nevertheless useful to file away for future reference. It certainly seems, as I suspected, that there has been some kind of resurrection of the Moriarty network. Friend Moran is heavily involved but there also seems to be a mysterious woman in the mix somewhere. Some say she is Madame Defarge.'

'What! That dreadful woman from *A Tale of Two Cities?*'

Holmes smiled at my naivete. 'Not quite, Watson. It is a pseudonym for a woman who ran a gang of criminals in Paris a few years ago. She disappeared mysteriously. Some say she is dead; others that she moved her base of operations and took on a different persona. Soapy told me that there are those who suspect that she is now in league with Moran. But there are no definite facts. Just rumours.'

'Well, your suspicions that the phoenix of the Moriarty Organisation is rising from the ashes is something to concern us, surely.'

Holmes nodded. 'Up to a point, but a venomous creature without a head is not quite as dangerous or effective. Moriarty was the genius that shaped and controlled and inspired his nefarious crew. You need such a fellow to fully resuscitate and lead such an organisation.'

'Surely there is no belief that the Professor is actually still alive... that he survived?'

Holmes closed his eyes, his features taking on a pained

expression. 'Rumours again. Wishful thoughts. I cannot contemplate such a scenario.'

The words were uttered in such an emotional fashion that I knew it would be best not to press the matter further.

After a moment, Holmes opened his eyes, gave a heavy sigh, shaking off his air of gloom with a tight grin. 'In the meantime, I have my networks on the lookout, the Irregulars are briefed and we must wait for further developments while being like old Soapy: keeping alert and watchful. Now a wash, a change of clothes, and a light supper, I think.'

Despite the efforts of the police and some discreet enquiries made by Holmes, there had been no sign of Colonel Moran since his escape from custody. 'He's lying low somewhere, maybe on the Continent,' said Holmes, 'but he will emerge eventually and be about his mischief once more, and I will be ready for him.' These words were uttered with a sense of finality that told me that Holmes did not wish to discuss the matter until further information presented itself.

Those first few weeks of my return to Baker Street and taking up my old quarters again were very strange to me. It was like winding back the clock and returning to my previous life. At times it seemed that I had never been away from those familiar rooms. The years of Holmes's absence were simply a peculiar dream and I had just woken up to discover life as it had always been. Remarkably Holmes and I soon settled back into our familiar ways with ease and while there was something comforting about this, at the same time there was also, to my mind, something surreal about the experience. To some extent I put this down to the delayed shock of seeing my friend again after spending three years believing that he had perished at the Reichenbach Falls. Of course, the return from the dead of someone close to you is a universal wish fulfilment. Indeed, in the dark hours when my mind was fogged with sleep, I wondered if one day my Mary might walk through the door again. How wonderful that would be.

It did not take long for the word to get around that Mr Sherlock Holmes was back in London and in the detective business once more. Clients began to arrive at regular intervals with a range of conundrums for him to solve. There were no really interesting cases at first, but he was happy to tackle these mundane problems in order, as he put it, 'to help me get back into the old routines again.'

Nevertheless, I knew that the note claiming to be from Moriarty continued to haunt Holmes. On first receiving it, he had examined it carefully, sniffing it and holding it up to the light before placing it carefully on his chemical bench. Late that night I saw him performing various tests and examining the fine grain of the heavy paper both with his lens and under the microscope. It tantalised him, and I had refrained from questioning him about it too much as I could see that his mind was whirling.

On one occasion when I returned from my club, I caught him staring at it as a wary zookeeper might look at a particularly deadly snake.

'Well, what have you learned?' I asked.

'First, tell me what *you* make of it,' he replied, handing it to me with reverential distaste.

'I cannot say with any certainty. I have not looked at it in detail and with such an expert eye as yourself.'

'But your impressions, my dear fellow. I would find them most useful. There is something about it which eludes me. A fresh perspective...'

Taking hold of the note and studying it for a few moments, I attempted to emulate my friend's methods.

'The paper is obviously expensive – its weight and fine grain say as much. There is a faint watermark which I cannot decipher. I cannot tell whether the handwriting is that of a man or a woman, but they have made no attempt to disguise it, and it has a marked quality of aggressiveness. The pressure of the nib on the paper has made indentations in places – particularly when writing your name.'

Holmes shuddered. 'Well observed. And you are correct about the paper, Watson. It is costly but not extravagant in design. No borders, subtle marbling or any of the touches of the nouveau riche. The watermark is the insignia of Maquet. It is a French manufacturer of luxury stationery, established in Paris in 1841 by the Maquet brothers, Hector and Charles.'

'So the author is French?'

'Not necessarily. The paper is obtainable in this country at exclusive stationers. However, my enquiries regarding customers at such establishments have been unsuccessful.' Holmes glanced at the note again. 'The handwriting is interesting. It is a model of economy. It was written with speed. Notice the innovative, fluid shortcuts the writer has used. This person has moved far from the confines of classroom manuscript exercises and developed a most distinctive hand. We are dealing with someone of intelligence, clarity of thought and drive to succeed. However, these positive traits are tempered by the large signature in comparison with the main body of the writing, which speaks of arrogance, and the angular characteristics indicate a lack of warmth, and extreme selfishness, perhaps extending to violence.' Holmes paused and pursed his lips thoughtfully. 'I have to say the odd squareness of the vowels are to my eyes quite reminiscent of the writing of a certain Professor.'

'You do not think that you might be thinking too much of Moriarty and applying what you know of the man to this correspondent?'

Holmes gave me a wry smile. 'Perhaps, though I try never to let my strong feelings about the Professor interfere with my judgment.' He smiled. 'I would be a poor detective indeed if I allowed the persistent vision of his oscillating head to obscure the facts.'

He returned to the note, taking it from my hand and twirling it between his long fingers. 'I have analysed the ink. It is a fine blend of iron gall, less used these days due to the introduction of aniline dye inks and the steel nib. Our note was written with a quill, as iron gall ink clogs and corrodes the modern metal nibs. It is a choice, a studied and peculiarly old-fashioned statement, favoured by those with a leaning towards the past and having a taste for expensive antiques, the pen and ink drawings of the old masters, leather-bound books and manuscripts. Ink can be made from very few components in anywhere from the smallest back room to the largest manufacturers. I have identified hundreds of separate types of ink in this country alone, and have begun to extend my researches into Europe. The particular balance and chemical composition of this ink suggests that it is also French, or possibly German. The gender of the writer is a puzzle. It is in general a masculine hand but there are certain female touches in the flourishes.'

'Can we track the writer down?'

Holmes shook his head. 'There is too little to go on here. However, the information may come in useful at a later date. In the meantime, we shall have to wait. If this is some fellow pretending to be the ghost of Professor James Moriarty, he is playing very accurately pitched psychological games, and I am happy to wait until he shows his hand further.'

Chapter Three

From the journal of John H. Watson

One evening in early June as we sat quietly in our rooms, Holmes consulting one of his old files and me riffling through the pages of the latest issue of *The Lancet*, I returned with a touch of trepidation to the topic of the note.

'Do you really think there is any possibility that Professor Moriarty could be alive? I sense that you have been harbouring such thoughts.'

Holmes stared at me for some moments with an intense expression on his hawk-like features before responding to my query.

'I have turned this matter over in my mind many times since receiving that wretched missive and hearing about the rumours that Soapy mentioned. However, the notion of Moriarty's survival is ridiculous. I saw him tumble over the precipice. I watched him fall, heard him scream all the way down until the thick spray hid him from view in a watery shroud.' He paused for a moment and turned his gaze to the empty grate, clenching his fists as he did so.

'And yet...' he continued, slowly measuring out the words, 'and yet they never found a corpse. There is no physical evidence of his death.'

'But no man could survive such a drop,' I said. 'His body would have been smashed to pieces in the rocks at the base of the Falls.'

Holmes nodded. 'Of course. And yet that cursed message introduced a note of doubt in my mind which I am finding difficult to shake off.' He gave a wry grin. 'The Professor haunted me for some time before his death and now it seems he is doing so from beyond the grave.'

'Remember, your old adage,' I said solemnly, 'In detective work "no ghosts need apply". I suggest you apply that maxim to this matter. Corpse or no corpse, Moriarty is dead and let that be an end of it.'

'Wise words, Watson. I can always rely on you to provide a down-to-earth practical solution. I will take your advice and endeavour to cast such thoughts from my mind. In truth my brain needs stimulus to crowd out such considerations. I need a challenging case, a seriously tangled skein to engage my mind; a real three-pipe problem.'

We had not long to wait for such a mystery to present itself.

The following day, Billy brought up a visiting card from a lady requiring Holmes' assistance in 'a desperate matter', the boy said, repeating her words. Holmes asked for the visitor to be admitted.

Some moments later, an elderly woman with a slightly stooped frame entered our sitting room with the assistance of a stick. A frilly bonnet sat uneasily on her lank grey hair. Her face was gaunt, but she wore an expression of strong determination. It was clear to me that in her youth she must have been quite a beautiful woman, but age had wrought its cruel way with her features. She was breathing heavily, as though the assault of the seventeen steps up to our rooms had been a great strain on her constitution. I moved forward and, gently taking her by the arm, led her to a comfortable chair.

'Thank you, young man,' she said, once she was seated, her voice husky and strained. 'I have come to see Mr Sherlock Holmes...'

'I am Holmes,' said my friend, taking a seat opposite the lady. 'How may I be of assistance?'

'By saving my brother's life.'

At the delivery of this melodramatic statement, Holmes' expression did not change. He had heard many similar pleas in his time as a detective. 'Perhaps you had better give me all the details,' he said quietly, steepling his fingers.

'Allow me to introduce myself: I am Elizabeth Courtney. I am a spinster and live in the family home, Ashtree House in Chiswick, with my brother, Arthur. He also is unmarried.' At this point she allowed herself a little smile. 'Indeed, I do believe that some of our neighbours are under the impression that we are man and wife, despite the fact that my brother is some fifteen years younger. Although Arthur and I are close, we are quite different characters. I am a shy, introverted individual who has spent a lifetime keeping my own counsel and being happy to do so. I suppose it is because of my quiet nature that I have never married, although I have to say, Mr Holmes, that it is not something I have ever desired. One of my blessings is that I am content with my own company. By contrast, Arthur is an outgoing society animal. He was a wild young man, burning the candle, as you might say, at both ends. He indulged in many amorous affairs, although none resulted in wedlock. He was also reckless at the gambling table and began associating with a decadent crowd, which led him further astray. Despite my efforts, taking on the role of motherly guardian rather than sister, to try to help keep him on the straight and narrow, I feel I have been far from successful in this matter. I am afraid to say that even the onset of middle age has not lessened his rash proclivities. Indeed, they seem to have increased in the last few years. I am ashamed to say that he has added drug-taking to his peccadillos, spending nights away from home in one of the opium dens in the East End. Despite my pleas to control this habit, it would seem that the drug has him in its power.'

'What is his employment, his source of income?' enquired Holmes.

'Our parents left us very well provided for financially and although Arthur squanders most of his allotted monthly income, he does occasionally find himself in funds from his gambling. He veers from abundance of cash to penury on a regular basis. When the latter state occurs, he comes to me for assistance, which, of course, I provide. Despite his dissipated behaviour, he is my brother and I love him.'

I sympathised with the plight of this sensitive old lady but I could not help thinking that her actions, her kindness towards her brother, had only encouraged his reckless ways. Sometimes it is wise to be cruel in order to be kind. I could see from Holmes' expression that he shared the same view.

'Telling you all this is very difficult for me,' Miss Courtney continued. 'Washing my dirty linen in public, as it were. I have never discussed Arthur's indiscretions with anyone before.'

'If I am to help you, I must know everything, but be assured that what you say to us in this room will go no further,' said Holmes.

'I thank you for that,' she said before turning to me. 'I wonder if I could trouble you for a glass of water.'

'Of course,' I said reaching for the gasogene and filling a small tumbler.

'Thank you.' After taking a series of sips, Miss Courtney resumed her narrative.

'Now I come to the heart of the matter. The reason that has forced me to seek help. I am at my wits' end as to what to do. As I mentioned earlier, Arthur has taken to visiting an opium den in Limehouse to smoke the dreadful concoction on sale there. I am not quite sure where it is located or exactly what it is called, although I did hear Arthur mumble the word "gold" in reference to it on one occasion when he arrived home late after one of his sessions in a somewhat confused state.'

Holmes shot me a knowing glance but said nothing, allowing the lady to continue her narrative uninterrupted.

'Sometimes he will stay away from home for two or three days at a time. When he returns he is in a wretched condition and takes to his bed for twenty-four hours or so, until the drug has left his system. However, he has now been gone for nearly a week. As yesterday dawned, I was beside myself with worry. I feared some terrible accident had occurred. One reads of such foul deeds in that disreputable part of London. I wondered for instance if he had fallen victim to footpads. Murdered maybe for the contents of his wallet. In such circumstances the imagination conjures up all sort of dark scenarios.'

'But something has happened to change your mind regarding these fears,' observed Holmes, smoothly.

Miss Courtney's eyes widened in surprise. 'Why yes, Mr Holmes, how did you know?'

Holmes pursed his lips. 'A simple assumption. Pray continue.'

'I really was at a loss what to do. I had no way of knowing where this dreadful drug den was and I certainly felt I could not go to the police for help in case I got my brother into trouble in some way. I would have to reveal his addiction. His reputation, the consequences... And then... and then...' The lady paused, her eyes welled with tears and she searched desperately in her reticule for a handkerchief.

Holmes said nothing and simply waited for her to control herself. My heart went out to her and I felt I should do something to ease her distress, but I could gauge from Holmes' stoical expression that he would consider any such action on my part to be ill-advised.

After a pause, Holmes repeated the last words of his client. 'And then...?'

'And then in yesterday's afternoon post, I received this letter.' She extracted the missive from her reticule and passed it to Holmes. He read it quickly, and then examined the paper, at one point lifting it up to the light and then holding it close to his nose before passing it to me.

I perused the scrawl, which I surmised was perpetrated by an uneducated hand:

'We have your brother in our power. For the moment he is safe but under restraint. We require you to furnish us with a ransom of five thousand pounds or we will cut his throat and deposit his body in the Thames. Be assured this is no idle threat. We will give you three days to organise your finances and then be in touch again to instruct you how to hand over the money. A final warning – do not contact the police or any independent investigator regarding this matter. If you do, it will be the worse for your brother.'

'I simply could not just do nothing about this,' said Miss Courtney, 'despite the threat in the letter. That is why I come to you. I felt that you could make discreet enquiries, discover where my brother is and who his captors are. You are my only hope. Can you help me, Mr Holmes?'

My friend stroked his chin and re-read the note. 'There is very little to go on, I'm afraid. The note provides no clues. The paper is cheap, easily obtainable from a number of stationers. The message has been written with a simple pen, the sort one finds in a post office, and is not likely to be owned by the correspondent. Do you have the envelope...?'

'Why yes.' Miss Courtney extracted it from her bag and passed it to Holmes.

'Postmarked Trafalgar Square. No help there.' He held the envelope close to his nose. 'Ah, the faint aroma of oriental spices. That could be a link to the opium den to which you referred. Very well, Miss Courtney, I will do what I can to throw some light on this dark business, but I warn you that in no way can I guarantee success. There are few crumbs at this table. However, leave the matter in my hands for a day and I will see what I can do.'

Our client beamed. 'Oh, Mr Holmes, I am so grateful.'

'Please save your gratitude until such a time when it becomes appropriate. This case is a difficult one with no guiding lights to lead the way.'

'I understand. But I have great faith in you.'

'Do you have a photograph of your brother?'

'Indeed I do. It is not a recent one I'm afraid, it was taken some ten years ago.' She produced a sepia cabinet photograph and passed it to Holmes, who studied it for a short time before handing it to me. A plump-faced fellow in possession of light-coloured curly hair, a pleasing countenance and a winning smile stared back at me from the thin piece of photographic cardboard. However, these open features were marred by what appeared to be a port wine stain shaped like a large tear drop on his right cheek. This blemish, a medical condition known as *nevus flammeus*, is caused by a vascular anomaly – a capillary malformation in the skin. Despite this mark on his face, I could easily see how this Arthur Courtney would have winning ways with the ladies. If anything, this slight disfigurement of his features may well in a strange way enhance his attractiveness. At the time the photograph was taken I estimated that he would be in his mid-thirties.

'Do you know of any friend or associate of your brother who may have accompanied him when visiting Limehouse?' asked Holmes.

Miss Courtney shook her head. 'I am afraid not. He kept that part of his life most secret. He never invited any of his friends to the house, so as a result I have no detailed knowledge of his acquaintances.'

'In that case,' said Holmes, 'I think I am in possession of all the information you can supply, unless there is anything else you think I should know.'

Miss Courtney thought for a moment and then shook her head. 'I fear not,' she said.

My friend rose from his chair. 'Very well. If you will call back here at five o'clock tomorrow afternoon, I will report back on any progress made. I have your address here on your card should I need to get in touch with you before then. And, of course, if you receive any further communications from the kidnappers, please inform me at once, no matter whether it be day or night.'

'I understand. I feel somewhat easier in my mind now that you are looking into the matter.'

Once the lady had left, Holmes threw himself back in his chair and burst out laughing.

I was shocked and bewildered by his behaviour. 'What on earth's the matter, Holmes?' I cried with concern.

'Oh, Watson, I am just relishing that masterful performance.'

'Performance? You mean the old lady, our client?'

'Old lady be blowed.' He rose swiftly from his chair, moved to the window and gazed down into the street below. With a wave of his outstretched hand, he beckoned me to join him.

'Look, look,' he cried as we observed our visitor leaving and making her way to a waiting cab at the kerbside.

Holmes chuckled heartily. 'She is certainly moving with much more ease and alacrity now. Observe – no stiff joints or stooping shoulders.'

I saw Miss Courtney, with a very sprightly gait, step into the cab. 'What does it mean?' I asked.

'Oh, my dear Watson, did you not see through the smoke and mirrors?' With another guffaw, he returned to his chair and flung himself down with gay abandon. 'We have just witnessed a brilliant, though flawed, performance, worthy of the great Ellen Terry herself.'

I shook my head in some confusion. 'I don't understand.'

'We have not been in the company of an elderly spinster, my friend. She was a much younger woman. I doubt if she has reached the age of thirty yet.'

I brought an image of our new client to mind. 'Surely you must be mistaken...'

'Makeup, dress and demeanour can be very convincing in creating a character, as I know personally. However, one must guard against chinks in the armour. In increasing maturity, it easy to use makeup to add to one's features, but the lady failed to pay attention to her hands, those smooth hands of a young woman. The teeth also – did you notice – pearly white, unlike the stained victims of an older person. I took note, too, of her clothes: they were brand new as though they hadn't been worn before. They probably hadn't. No doubt purchased for this premiere performance. The dress had been padded to disguise her youthful figure. This became obvious to me when she leaned forward to extract the letter from her handbag. The material moved in a most unnatural fashion. The walking stick, too, had not been used. Did you not notice the brass ferule? Bright and shiny with no scuffs and marks one sees on a stick that is in constant use. Her entrance into our room was a little overdone, all that heavy breathing and slow arthritic movement. No sign of that once she left the building. You saw how she virtually skipped her way to the waiting cab.'

I must confess I had been utterly taken in by the Courtney woman. She had convinced me completely. 'Why the deception? What is it all about, Holmes?' I asked.

My friend shrugged his shoulders. 'It is too soon to say. But it was a deliberate charade concocted to puzzle me. It is obvious to me that I was meant to penetrate the disguise and realise that our elderly lady was an imposter. The teeth could easily have been darkened, gloves could have been worn to disguise the youthful hands but they were deliberately on show. It was her intention that I should see through the artifice. It was all deliberate in order to tantalise me.

'Then why on earth didn't you challenge her – expose the charade?' I asked, somewhat puzzled.

Holmes smiled. 'Because the game would end there. It is clear that there is much more to this tempting and blatant deception, which was enacted to intrigue me. I did not intend to cut it off in its prime. There is more to this than meets the eye. Well, certainly the lady has been successful in her goal: I am intrigued. It seems like some sort of game, but its motive is not yet clear. However, I am convinced that she is hoping to lure me into it for some dark purpose.'

'Shouldn't you attempt to follow the cab then?'

'Certainly not. That is no doubt what they expect me to do.'

'They?'

'Of course, there are bound to be others involved, including that so-called brother of hers, Arthur.'

'So-called.'

'It is highly likely he is just an accomplice in this dark charade and no relation whatsoever.' At this juncture, Holmes picked up the cabinet photograph. 'Did you not notice the identification of the photographic studio printed at the bottom: Royal Images of Oxford Street?'

I nodded. 'Well, yes I saw that. Is it relevant?'

'Indeed. I know the establishment. As you are aware, I keep a keen eye of the various businesses in London. As a consulting detective in this great city it is important that I note all changes and developments that take place. How else am I able to function effectively? You never know when such information may come in useful – as now. I know that Royal Images was established one year before I disappeared from London. That was four years ago and therefore the photograph of Arthur Courtney – for such we must refer to him at the moment – could not have been taken ten years ago, as we were told. I think it is safe to say that this is a recent picture and that he is probably about the same age as his so-called "sister", Elizabeth: in his thirties.'

'It is very confusing and baffling. I must confess I am all at sea with this matter as you explain it.'

'Do not take it too much to heart, Watson. Although I have deduced a number of facts from our interview with the lady who calls herself Elizabeth Courtney, I am as yet unable to construct a logical scenario. One thing is for certain, we were visited by a young woman in an obvious disguise and told a pack of lies in order to stimulate my curiosity: cheese for the detective mouse. All I surmise – rather than deduce – is that she and her cohorts want to draw me in to something which has all the suggestions of a trap.'

'What do you intend to do?'

'Make my way very cautiously into it. I will treat this investigation as a genuine one.'

'This sounds dangerous, Holmes. What will be your first move?'

'Our client has deliberately left two paths to follow. My instinct is to take the one that leads to Limehouse, which intrigues me more than the photographic studio. We can follow up on that later. An opium den? I cannot resist a touch of the dramatic. The lady very cunningly dropped the word "gold" when referring to it. This was an obvious reference to lead me to The Bar of Gold. As you know I am familiar with this establishment in Upper Swandam Lane. No doubt she was aware of this. Indeed, I shall begin there. I do not wish to disappoint her. In the meantime, you could be of assistance to me also, if you are willing.'

'Of course. What do you require me to do?'

'Take a trip out to Chiswick and have a look at Ashtree House from a distance. Do not enter the grounds. The address may well be a red herring; if so, we need to eliminate it from our investigations. See if you can fall into conversation with some locals and find out what they know about the inhabitants. Gossip is one of the greatest sources of information. But be discreet.'

'You can rely on me, Holmes.'

My friend rose hurriedly from his chair and made his way towards his bedroom. 'Good,' he cried. 'Let's be about it. The game's afoot!'

Chapter Four

As the woman calling herself Elizabeth Courtney stepped inside the waiting cab, the silhouetted figure sitting inside leaned forward, the pale bearded face caught in the shaft of daylight as the door opened, the thin lips forming a smile of greeting.

'How did it go, my dear?' he asked as the woman settled herself down and the cab began moving.

Elizabeth Courtney grinned. 'Like a dream. I could see from his face and demeanour that Holmes picked up on all the weaknesses in my story and my disguise. I am convinced that he is well aware that I am no wrinkled old spinster and that my tale of woe is a work of pure fiction.'

'Excellent,' said her companion.

'I am sure that our detective friend will now be suitably intrigued and allow his caution to weaken. It will not be very long before he steps onto my web, and we shall be waiting.

Slowly, slowly, catchee Sherlock.'

They both laughed as the cab rattled through the streets of London.

Chapter Five

Sherlock Holmes decided to use a minimal disguise for his visit to The Bar of Gold. He knew that the clientele of the establishment was mixed; from smart businessmen of the city to a variety of tradesmen and indeed scruffy beggars who had scooped up enough coins to buy themselves a pipe. He was well aware that he would fit in easily merely by donning a shabby suit of the kind that would be worn by a shop worker, whitening his features and adding dark circles under his eyes to suggest that he was a regular opium user. Satisfied with his appearance, he set off for Limehouse.

As he approached The Bar of Gold, he was reminded of the last time he had visited the premises in the case of the man with the twisted lip. Upper Swandam Lane was a vile alley lurking behind the high wharves which line the north side of the river to the east of London Bridge. Even at this time of day – mid-afternoon – street women were plying their desperate trade, drunken ruffians dozed in dilapidated doorways and the tangible stench of decay hung in the air. The drug den was situated between a slop shop and a gin shop and approached by a steep flight of stairs leading down to a black gap like the mouth of a cave.

Holmes descended the dank stairway, opened the rough wooden door and entered. The extensive chamber was filled with rows of wooden bunks on three levels, most of which were filled with prone individuals, wretched souls enslaved to the power of the poppy. Some were lying on their backs smoking, while others resembling gaunt corpses were sleeping off the drug. The air was thick with the powerful smell and thin brown mist of opium smoke.

He was approached by the gatekeeper of the establishment, a tall Chinese man in a long oriental gown. He bowed gently. 'Welcome. A pipe for you, sir.'

Holmes knew that at this juncture that he had to carry on with the charade. 'Yes,' he said, adopting a gruff throaty voice. 'How much?'

The man held up a metal pipe, the small bowl already prepared with the drug. 'Three shillings, if you please,' came the smooth reply.

Holmes handed over coins and took the pipe.

His host bowed again and waved his arm in the direction of an empty bunk. Holmes made his way through the gloom, lay down on the bunk and lit the pipe. He knew that he should appear to take a few inhalations to be convincing as an addict and justify his presence in this adjunct of Hell. He gazed around him and through the gloom he caught glimpses of bodies lying in strange and fantastic poses, bowed shoulders, bent knees, heads thrown back and chins pointing upwards, with here and there a dark lacklustre eye turned on him. Holmes performed the pantomime of puffing on the pipe, before lying back on the sacking and gradually feigning unconsciousness.

He laid there for an hour before he felt a hand upon his shoulder. He opened his eyes and gazed upon the smiling face of his host. 'Another pipe?' he said.

Holmes rolled his eyes as though trying to focus on the world once more. 'No, no. I... have little money to spare.'

'Another time, perhaps,' he said, mildly disappointed that he could not make another sale.

Suddenly Holmes sat up and grabbed the man's sleeve. 'I need help. Can you help me?' His voice emerged as a hoarse whisper.

A look of bewilderment passed over the man's features but he said nothing.

Holmes thrust his hand into his jacket pocket and produced the photograph of Arthur Courtney. 'I am looking for this man. He owes me money. If I can find him, I can enjoy more smokes. Do you recognise him? I know he comes here.' He thrust the photograph close to the man's face. He studied it for a short time before he gave a gentle shrug of the shoulders.

'We have many clients here. All look the same to me.'

Holmes scrabbled in his pocket and produced a florin, which glinted in the gloom. 'My last coin,' he gasped. It is yours if you can help me. Look, look again. The blonde hair. The birthmark.'

With some reluctance the man gazed at the photograph again and then nodded his head. 'Yes, I think I have seen him. The stain on his face...'

'Has he been in here recently?'

There was a pause before he replied. 'Yes. He has business with the boss.'

'Your boss.'

A nod of assertion. 'Li Tang.'

'Where is he now?'

'I am afraid I cannot say.'

'This man with the mark on his face – he is a threat to Li Tang. I must see him and pass on a warning. It will be bad for you if I do not see Li Tang.'

'I do not know… I…' There was fear in his voice as he uttered these words. Suddenly a dark figure appeared behind him and placed a long taloned hand on his shoulder.

'Back to your duties,' came a rich, cultured voice from the darkness. 'I will deal with this matter.'

The host turned to face the speaker, gave a strangled squawk of horror and hurried away.

'I believe you wish to see me. I am Li Tang.' He stepped closer to Holmes and his features were illuminated by the amber glow of a nearby candle. The man had a gaunt, sallow face, thin lips and fiercely penetrating eyes, each of a different colour: one grey and one brown. He wore a small diamond earring in his right ear and his long shiny black hair was swept back away from the face and tied in a pigtail down his back. There was something about his demeanour and appearance that chilled Holmes. He knew instinctively that this was a man to be wary of – even a man to fear.

'Perhaps you would like to like to continue our conversation in my office at the rear of these premises, Mr Holmes. It will afford us privacy and more comfort for you than a bed of straw.'

'That would be most amenable,' replied Holmes suavely, raising an eyebrow.

'Good. If you please, follow me.'

Holmes swung his legs over the edge of the bunk and stood up.

'This way, Mr Holmes,' said Li Tang, his mouth stretched into a wide grin, which exposed a row of tiny white teeth. 'We have been expecting you.'

Chapter Six

From the journal of John H. Watson

It did not take me long to locate Ashtree House in a quiet road off the main thoroughfare in Chiswick. It was a substantial detached property of fairly recent vintage. I gazed at it through the closed iron gates. There was no sign of life within or without the property. The darkened windows stared back at me blankly. I also noted that the lawn fronting the bay window was overgrown and the flowerbeds seemed somewhat neglected. I was mindful of Holmes' instructions that I was not, under any circumstances, to approach the house or try to gain entry by fair means or foul.

'Can I help you?' came a voice from behind me.

I turned and faced a tall, smartly dressed middle-aged gentleman who had a curly-haired spaniel in tow, pulling eagerly on its leash.

'I was just admiring the house. It is the sort of property I am looking for.'

'Well, I believe you are in luck. I can tell you it is for sale. It has been empty for some months.'

'Empty,' I repeated, failing to keep the surprise out of my voice.

'Yes, the previous owner, a doctor and his wife, moved away some months ago to Scotland, Edinburgh to be precise. I knew the family well. I was very sad to see them go. They were a charming couple. I live in the house next door. I have the address of the agents who handle this property if you are interested. I don't like living next to an empty building and it would be nice to see it occupied as a home again.'

I realised that I had to keep up my charade and nodded with enthusiasm. 'That would be most helpful,' I said, making some enquiries about the neighbourhood and the configuration of the interior.

'Would you mind taking charge of Gladstone while I retrieve the details?' he asked, thrusting the leash in my direction. I did as he requested and patted the dog on the head while its owner extracted his wallet from inside his coat. He handed me a business card with the name and address of the estate and land agents in Piccadilly. 'They will be able to assist you with your enquiries.'

'Thank you,' I said slipping the card into my breast pocket. 'Tell me, sir, do you know of anyone in the neighbourhood called Courtney – an Elizabeth and Arthur Courtney. A brother and sister or husband and wife. The gentleman has a birth mark on his right cheek.'

My companion did not have to consider this question for long. He very promptly gave me a firm shake of the head. 'I have lived in this area for five years and I know of no one who matches your description,' he said, taking hold of the dog's leash again.

'Ah, well, no matter. Thank you for your information,' I said with a smile, patting my breast pocket.

We parted company and I made my way back towards the

underground station frustrated and annoyed. The excursion to Chiswick had in the end been a fool's errand. The woman calling herself Elizabeth Courtney certainly had presented us with a very large pack of lies. No doubt Holmes had sent me off on what had been a fruitless mission just to make absolutely sure nothing the woman had said bore any truth. He was using me to double check that the address in Chiswick had no real connection with the Courtney mystery at all, and certainly that appeared to be the case.

On my return to Baker Street, Mrs Hudson emerged from her sitting room as I entered the hallway. 'Oh, Dr Watson, there's been a delivery for Mr Holmes,' she said.

'A delivery?'

'Yes, a large cabin trunk. It was brought here about an hour ago, marked fragile and addressed for the personal attention of Sherlock Holmes.'

'Really? I had no idea that Holmes was expecting such a delivery. Where is the trunk now?'

'I had the men take it up to your sitting room. It was a heavy thing. It took both of them to get it up the stairs.'

I thanked Mrs Hudson for this information and then made my way up to our sitting room. On entering, I discovered the large trunk on the hearthrug. It was a normal, sturdy and somewhat battered cabin trunk, with a curved lid and, as Mrs Hudson had informed me, had a large address label bearing Holmes' name. Slipping off my hat and coat, I poured myself a brandy, sat in my old chair and gazed at the trunk. Its presence in the room was almost hypnotising. I stared at it with growing speculation. What did it contain? Had Holmes ordered some piece of equipment to add to his other scientific paraphernalia? It was possible, although he had made no mention of it to me. Well, I reasoned, however intrigued I was by the trunk, I would have to wait for my friend's return before my curiosity was satisfied.

Chapter Seven

ᘒ

Li Tang led Sherlock Holmes into a small chamber situated at the rear of The Bar of Gold. It glowed with dim lantern light and was exquisitely furnished in the oriental style. Near the far wall was an ornate desk. Li Tang made a move to sit behind it and then suddenly changed his mind and approached a cabinet nearby which had an array of bottles and glasses.

'You would perhaps care for a glass of rice wine, Mr Holmes?'

Holmes gave a thin smile. 'I think not. Partaking of liquid on these premises may be a little foolhardy.'

'Oh, I see. You fear that you may be poisoned.'

'Something of that nature.'

'I can assure you, my wine is of the finest vintage and quite unsullied by unwanted ingredients. I am not here to harm you, Mr Holmes. I am merely a courier. A well-paid courier. I simply have something to pass on to you, vouchsafed to me by a third party.'

'Which third party?'

Li Tang smiled mischievously. 'As you may deduce, I am not at liberty to reveal that information. It would, as they say, be more than my life is worth. However, I can tell you that I was informed that you would visit these premises in search of someone and, when you arrived, I was to pass on something to you and then, with great courtesy, bid you farewell.'

'What is it that you have to give to me?'

Li Tang moved to his desk and picked up a small ebony box and handed it to Holmes who, with caution, removed the lid. It contained a folded sheet of ivory writing paper but sitting on top of it was a small scorpion.

With a shocked gasp, Holmes paused for a second to observe the motionless creature inside, before snapping the lid shut, flipping the catch and placing the box on top of a japanned desk in the corner of the room.

Li Tang laughed. 'So the great Sherlock Holmes can be fearful – even of a lifeless thing.'

'Self-preservation makes for swift reactions,' responded Holmes tartly. 'Death comes in many disguises.' He leaned forward and picked up the sheet of paper that had fallen from the box. Unfolding it, there was a handwritten message:

'Well done, Sherlock. You have absorbed the rules of the game and you have been successful. However, you must learn to be more cautious – consider if the scorpion had been alive... But that would have been too easy. Nevertheless, this is a deadly game – one I am determined that you will lose. Are you ready for the next throw of the dice?

Sincerely yours,

Moriarty.'

At the sight of the signature, the distinctive hand and strong brownish black ink, the hairs on the back of Holmes's neck prickled and he felt his blood run cold. This was ridiculous. The writer of the note, the creator of this bizarre scenario, could not possibly be Professor James Moriarty. He was dead.

Wasn't he?

Sometime later, Holmes was sitting in the gloom of a hansom cab on his way back to Baker Street. His mind was awhirl with thoughts relating to the events of the day. He recalled in detail the visit to his sitting room of the creature calling herself Elizabeth Courtney and the creative fiction she spewed forth. Some aspects of her narrative were so risible as to be designed deliberately in order for him to smell that very pungent rat she was dangling before his nose. He knew he was being led to The Bar of Gold and he felt fairly certain that the so-called brother was also a red herring, a lure to take him to the premises at Upper Swandam Lane, but he had been surprised at the outcome of his visit to the drug den.

This was what annoyed and frustrated him: at present he had no idea what connected the whole scenario. Some kind of game it would seem, as the note suggested, but for what purpose he could not yet surmise. If the enemy, for so he must regard the Courtney woman, wished to harm him, kill him, such an event could so easily have been arranged in the smoky shadows of The Bar of Gold, an establishment where death was no stranger. It was clear to him that Li Tang was as he had described himself – merely a paid agent and not a major player in the game. He had been lured up a blind alley apparently for the amusement of someone who professed to be Moriarty, to demonstrate to him how easy it was to move him around, like a piece on a chessboard.

Could it be that Elizabeth Courtney was actually the puppet

master? At this thought, another struck him as his mind wandered back to the original note and its French connection. The real identity of his tormentor was the puzzling element of the affair that piqued him and gnawed away at his intellect. However, he knew that for the moment, until the mist cleared, he would have to play the game her way. One thing was certain, the matter was not over; there was more to this challenging conundrum yet to come.

Part Three

The Game Grows Darker

Chapter Eight

From the journal of John H. Watson

It had been a dull cloudy day and the shadows were already lengthening into evening as I heard the familiar tread of my friend Sherlock Holmes upon the stairs leading up to our sitting room. As soon as he entered, I saw from the grim expression of disappointment on his face indicating that his visit to The Bar of Gold had not borne fruit.

'By your demeanour, I assume that your investigations have been as singularly unsuccessful as my own.'

Holmes gave me a bleak smile. '"Singularly unsuccessful". You old literary gent. What a way you have with words. Precise, succinct and accurate. Yes, singularly unsuccessful sums up my excursion admirably, although there was a surprising development – details of which can be discussed later. I have an ebony box and a dead scorpion to examine, though I am confident that they will reveal nothing useful, but at the moment I am more curious about this.' He pointed at the chest on the hearth rug.

'It was delivered when we were out. It is addressed to you. I thought perhaps it contained some specialist item you have ordered.'

Holmes shook his head. 'I was expecting no such delivery. Allow me to get out of these disreputable clothes – they reek of opium – and I will investigate further.'

Some ten minutes later, dressed in his usual sombre attire, he returned to the sitting room and, picking up his magnifying glass from the side table, he knelt down by the chest and examined it closely. 'Interesting, though elementary,' he murmured. 'It provides the basis for several simple deductions.'

'Such as...?

'It has been stored for some time in a damp cellar: the metal corner pieces on the base are tinged with rust. It is of sturdy construction, an elegant piece, in fact, and therefore would have cost a pretty penny when it was originally purchased, which seems to suggest that the owner is comfortably off and indeed can afford to use such a trunk as a conveyance.'

'You have no idea of the sender or its contents.'

'Certainly not the contents,' he observed slowly after a brief pause. 'However, the writing on the label, although printed in capitals, bears a similarity in the shaping of the letters and the colour of the ink to those of the warning letter that Lestrade brought to our notice. As to what the trunk holds... Let us make that discovery, shall we? If you would be so good as to pass me the jack knife from the mantel...'

I did as requested and Holmes cut the ropes that were securing it.

'Now then... what have we here?' he said, flipping the metal catch and raising the lid.

Peering inside the trunk, I gave a gasp of horror. Curled up in a foetal position was a dead body. Holmes said nothing, but I could tell from his expression and wide-eyed gaze that he was as stunned as I by the grisly contents.

Gently he pulled back the lolling head of the corpse to reveal its features and there was another shock awaiting us. There before us was the plump face with the disfiguring port wine stain and thatch of blonde curly hair which we had seen in a photograph earlier that day. This, then, was the man we had been told was Arthur Courtney.

Chapter Nine

From the journal of John H. Watson

'The poor devil,' I cried, as we stared down at the crumpled corpse in the trunk on our hearth rug.

'Indeed,' replied my friend, pulling out his lens and carefully registering every aspect of the poor man's position. 'An unfortunate pawn in the fiendish game. Help me lift him out so we can examine him more closely – establish the cause of death and discover what clues his clothes and body may reveal.'

We laid him out on the floor and then moved the trunk to one side so we could get a better look at him.

'How long do you think he has been dead?' asked Holmes as he began to probe the man's pockets.

Gently I turned the head from side to side with comparative ease, although it was a little stiff. It was at the point where rigor mortis had begun to set in but the movement was still flexible. 'It is difficult to be accurate but I would suspect between three to four hours.'

'So he could well have been alive when that lady calling herself

Elizabeth Courtney was in our rooms.'

'It is most likely.'

'The clothes have been stripped of all personal items apart from this gold watch, which is inscribed to Arthur Richard Courtney on his twenty-first birthday, 1865. The engraving is aged sufficiently to prove that the date is original. Thus, Courtney is his real name and this timepiece no doubt belonged to his father.'

'So one part of that fairy tale concoction was true after all.'

'It would seem so, and that could be an error of judgement on the part of our enemy,' he said, slipping the watch into his own coat pocket.

'Have you any notion of how he was murdered?'

'Indeed.' Producing a pair of tweezers from his waistcoat pocket, Holmes leaned forward and reaching behind the dead man's ear extracted what looked like a small thorn. I held out my hand to examine it, but Holmes halted my actions. 'Don't touch it, Watson, the tip is poisoned. See...' He pointed to the nape of the neck below the ear. There was a tiny speck of blood, which indicated where the puncture had been.

'The tip was probably doctored by some poisonous concoction: swift acting and deadly.'

'Strychnine, perhaps?'

Holmes nodded. 'Possibly. From the man's features there is evidence of the muscle spasms typical of this particular substance. The tightening of the jaw: *risus sardonicus*. And traces of the facial congestion associated with asphyxia. Poison at any rate.'

'This mystery grows darker and more puzzling,' I said. 'Why use something so arcane as a poisoned dart?'

'Our antagonist obviously has a theatrical bent. Dark it is meant to appear, but nevertheless I now begin to perceive that there is a linear thread running through this affair. I just need to grasp it and all will become clear.'

As he spoke there were raucous sounds, raised voices and heavy footsteps outside our rooms. In an instant the door burst open and a red-faced burly constable entered, followed by a tall, gaunt, mealy-mouthed individual, wearing a long pale brown raincoat. He stepped forward in a forceful, arrogant manner and spotting the body on the floor gave a sharp cry, a mixture of shock and delight.

'Ah, ah!' he crowed. 'Caught red-handed, as it were. Mr Sherlock Holmes, I am arresting you for murder – for the murder of this... this individual.'

Holmes chuckled. 'You are well prepared,' he said casually, 'for I see that you have the warrant already in your hand.'

'Indeed I have.'

'Inspector...?'

'Stead.'

Neither Holmes nor I had encountered this Scotland Yarder before but there was something oafish and belligerent in his demeanour that I found offensive. 'You are not suggesting that Sherlock Holmes is responsible for this man's death – for his murder,' I said with some heat.

'Well done, Doctor, that is exactly what I'm suggesting.'

'But this is ridiculous. Surely you know who Mr Holmes is?'

Stead smirked. 'Of course I do. He's the bloody know-it-all who thinks he's king of the private detectives. Well, that won't wash with me. I have received information that Mr Smarty Pants here has carried out the brutal murder of a certain Mr Arthur Courtney – who I assume is the poor devil sprawled on the floor there.'

'You seem to assume an awful lot,' observed Holmes, tartly. 'May I ask who has provided you with this information?'

Stead gave a brief rasping laugh. 'You may ask, but I have no intention of telling you. That will keep until the trial.'

It was now Holmes' turn to laugh. 'Ah, Inspector, I see that you have sketched out this farce to its conclusion. No doubt you contemplate seeing me on the gallows.'

Stead nodded forcefully. 'Certainly, that is the probable outcome,' came the smug response.

'But what is my motive? And how did this fellow die?'

Stead gave a quick glance at the corpse and a look of uncertainty flashed across his features.

'Mrs Hudson, our landlady, can vouch that this trunk was delivered to these premises a few hours ago,' I said.

'That's as maybe. No doubt a receptacle for the body to be transported elsewhere...'

'Oh, this is ridiculous,' I snapped. 'Why would Mr Holmes wish to murder a perfect stranger?'

Stead tapped his nose conspiratorially. 'We have ways of finding out such things down at the Yard. We too make our own "deductions", Doctor. You don't have a monopoly on solving mysteries, you know.'

I gave a snort of exasperation. The man was a fool. A fool, who no doubt saw this arrest as a significant feather in his cap if he could take into custody and prove the guilt of the foremost champion of law and order in the land.

Stead turned to the red-faced constable. 'Right, Johnson, put the darbies on him.'

The policeman pulled the handcuffs from his belt and made a move towards Holmes, but he, with the swiftness of a gazelle, leapt towards the mantelpiece, pulled out the jack knife that had been replaced there and grabbed Inspector Stead. Before the policeman knew what was happening Holmes had swung him round and held him in a stranglehold with the knife poised at his neck. Stead let out a croak of fear.

For an instant I was shocked at this violent action. Had Holmes lost his mind by attacking the policeman in this fashion?

'Fear not, Watson, these fellows are no more police officers than I am the man in the moon. Be a good chap and see to the so-called constable.'

I needed no further bidding. Snatching up the poker I turned and stepped towards the red-faced fellow. He emitted a cry of alarm and without a moment's hesitation, he turned on his heel and made a bolt for the door. Within seconds he was scrambling down the staircase, making good his escape. His cowardly panic amused me. His bulky stern exterior obviously concealed a very timid resolve.

Holmes now threw Stead into the wicker chair. The man had also lost his arrogant bluster, his features taut with worry. My friend stood over him, still wielding the knife.

'Now then, "Inspector", perhaps you will tell me who sent you and where you were going to take me.' He leaned further forward so that the tip of the knife was only inches from the man's throat.

'Don't hurt me, please,' Stead croaked.

'Whether I do or not remains to be seen,' said Holmes sternly. 'It all depends on how cooperative you are.'

Stead's face twitched with anguish as he nodded vigorously. 'I'll tell you all I know. Honest.'

'Who sent you here?'

Stead's eyes widened with fear and he wiped the perspiration from his top lip with the sleeve of his coat. 'I don't know his name,' he said. 'He just called himself "the Colonel". I'm an actor, you see, and he wanted me to play the part of a police inspector.'

'How did he get in touch with you?'

'I answered an advertisement in the press asking for a tall authoritative actor to take on the role of a police detective. There were quite a lot of applicants.'

'Where was this?'

'In a private room in the Goat and Compass – a public house in Streatham. That's where I met Sam Harper, my constable. He was employed the same day.'

Holmes' eyes glittered with interest at this revelation and he relaxed his hold of the knife. 'What was your brief? What did this Colonel ask you to do?'

'Well… we were to come here at an appointed time and arrest you for murder. He told us that there would be a body in the room but we were not to be alarmed by that. We were told it wasn't real. The whole thing was an elaborate joke… to embarrass you.'

'Didn't you think that the whole scenario was odd?' I asked.

Stead shifted his eyes nervously in my direction. 'I suppose I did, but the money was so good I let that go. I'd be working six months at least to earn as much as the Colonel promised me.'

'What were you supposed to do with me once you had me in your custody?' said Holmes.

'We had a cab waiting outside… and we were to transport you to a warehouse down by the docks. The Colonel would be waiting and we'd hand you over to him and that would be our job done. I've no idea what was to happen afterwards. If the truth be told…'

'Oh, yes, do let the truth be told,' murmured Holmes darkly.

Stead wiped the sleeve across his face. 'I didn't care to know what happened after we had delivered you into the hands of the Colonel. I'd played my part and I'd be happy to take my money and scarper.'

'Where exactly was this warehouse?'

'It was called Sullivan's down near the river on Bloxsome Street.'

'Sounds a charming venue, don't you think, Watson?'

'If you say so, Holmes.'

'Oh, I do, and I think we should take a trip there in the company of our thespian friend here.'

'No, no,' cried Stead, half rising from the chair. 'Please leave me out of it. Look, gents, I haven't committed any crime or brought harm to either of you. Please let me go. I beg of you.'

Holmes shook his head. 'I think you'll find that you are responsible for several offences. And your role in this drama is not yet complete.' With swift strides he moved to the window and gazed at the street below. 'Well, there is no cab waiting outside our premises now. No doubt your "constable" took advantage of it as a getaway vehicle. In all probability he is on his way to inform the Colonel of the bad news that his fake officers of the law have failed in their fake duties. Grab your coat, Watson. You and the reluctant Inspector Stead are about to join me in a visit to Sullivan's Warehouse on Bloxsome Street.'

Some moments later, the three of us went downstairs. Our new companion had lapsed into a sulky silence. His features registered how unhappy he was at his continued involvement in this venture but he was also well aware that he had no choice in the matter.

'Will you be a good fellow, Watson, and hail a cab for us? We will wait in the hallway here. I don't want to give our friend the opportunity to make a break for it. I am really not in the mood for haring down Baker Street in pursuit of a Scotland Yard imposter.'

I did as requested and quickly secured a hansom.

He and Stead left 221B and headed for the waiting cab.

Suddenly there was a loud crack similar to that of a branch

snapping from a tree. Stead gave a wheezy exhalation and his body lost its rigidity. As he began to crumple to the pavement, his eyes flickering wildly, I noticed a dark spot between his eyes. He had been shot in the head.

Chapter Ten

From the journal of John H. Watson

'Well, we have two dead bodies now,' I observed gloomily, as I stared at the corpse of the man who had called himself Inspector Stead. We had carried him upstairs into our sitting room and laid him on the chaise longue.

'Indeed,' responded Holmes with a sigh. 'Let us hope Mrs Hudson does not find out we are turning her abode into a charnel house. We will need to get these poor souls out of here as soon as possible. A telegram to Lestrade with the briefest of explanations should do the trick.'

'How did you know that Stead and the constable were imposters?'

'You mean apart from their rather over-the-top performances? It was mainly their feet.'

'Feet?'

'Official policemen, including inspectors, are issued with regulation boots. You'll have seen Lestrade's many times. Large cumbersome articles that make his presence known in advance as he clumps up our staircase. These fellows were wearing ordinary shoes and rather disreputable ones. Our friend Stead wore a grubby shirt which had, I observed, traces of make-up around the collar – theatrical make-up which suggested to me that the fellow was an actor. And the set of handcuffs were also not regulation issue. And, come now, Watson, would Scotland Yard send an inspector of whom I've never heard to arrest me for murder? It was clear to me that the scenario was some kind of obvious set-up.'

'I can see that now as you explain it, but it is all so mystifying. What on earth is going on here, Holmes? What does all this mean?'

'They are playing with me, Watson. They are deliberately trying to confuse me, to unbalance my equilibrium. But these two murders show they are deadly serious and dangerous.'

'But what is their purpose?'

He shrugged his shoulders. 'To addle my brain. To undermine my confidence. However, I am certain that these mind games will end in an attack upon my life. Someone is determined to destroy me, but they are doing it slowly in a cat and mouse fashion. A poisoned dart or a bullet in the head, a fate as befell these two fellows here, would be too easy, too simple. They mean to dangle me on their strings like a marionette until they feel it is time to cut them and I fall lifeless, no longer dancing to their tune.'

I shuddered at this thought. 'You say "they" – who are "they"?'

'One must assume that it is Colonel Moran and his cronies. He has carried his obsession to destroy me over the years, ever since Reichenbach. Stead mentioned that his employer called himself the Colonel. He suspected that this information would be passed to me as a tease. And yet all these shenanigans – distressed clients, bodies in trunks, actors impersonating policemen – that is not Moran's style. The old shikari lures his victim out into the open and fires.

A clean simple death. No, there is someone else involved in this business and it would seem to me that it is someone who bears a deep grudge against me. An individual who wants to unsettle me, frustrate me, demoralise me before administering the final blow.'

'Oh, Holmes, you are not thinking of Moriarty again.'

'I am resisting the temptation, but that fiery spark of doubt will not be doused.'

I shook my head in dismay. 'The fellow is dead,' I observed with emphasis.

'Of course, of course. You are quite right, Watson.' Holmes flashed me a smile, but I was not convinced by his words.

'What is our next move?' I asked attempting to return to practicalities.

'After we have informed Lestrade about our "visitors" here, I suggest we make a journey to Sullivan's warehouse. No doubt the plotters will have vacated the premises now that their machinations have come to naught, but two stealthy sleuths may be able to pick up a scent or a clue, probably something left deliberately to tease me. Are you game, old chap?'

'Of course. I want to be there when you finally unravel this strange mystery.'

'Excellent. May I add that I think it would be wise if you brought your revolver with you.'

The chimes of Big Ben were announcing the hour of ten o'clock as we crossed the river in a hansom. At Holmes' instructions, the cabbie dropped us at the corner of Bloxsome Street down by the docks. The area was deserted, not a sight or sound of any other individual in the area. The sky was clear and a newly minted moon shone down, providing sufficient illumination to aid us in our search for Sullivan's warehouse. As we moved down the narrow, cobbled thoroughfare, I caught a glimpse of the dark river some distance ahead of us, its undulating surface dappled with creamy moonlight.

Holmes stopped and raised his stick, pointing it at a low-roofed building on our right. 'There it is, Watson.'

The place was in total darkness and in my imagination the blackened windows, protected by a series of iron bars, were staring out at us in the moonlight with eerie malevolence. They seemed to be challenging us to enter. There were two large doors on the left side of the building which allowed access for deliveries and, on the right, what appeared to be an office door. We moved forward cautiously, Holmes retrieving his burgling kit from his overcoat pocket. However, as we reached the door, we observed a large white envelope pinned above the lock and the name SHERLOCK HOLMES in large capital letters inscribed upon it.

'You were expected,' I said.

'Of course I was,' Holmes replied, dislodging the envelope from its moorings and tearing open the flap. He extracted a sheet of paper and holding it close to his face read the contents. Emitting a sharp barking laugh, he passed the paper to me. I read the following: '*Congratulations, Mr Holmes. You seem to have won this round – but keep watching your back. M.*'

The letter 'M' sent a shiver down my spine. Had I been wrong all this time and was it as I suspected, as Holmes had feared, that Moriarty really was still alive? This thought flamed in my mind briefly, but I quickly removed it. Obviously, this was just another feature of this deadly game in which we were involved. Indeed, the 'M' could easily stand for Moran.

'What do we do now, Holmes?'

'We will take a cursory look around. However, I am sure there will be no clues that will aid us in tracking down the mysterious M. When their plan to capture me and transport me here fell through, they would have been away like the wind, removing all signs of their occupation. This is a formidable opponent and I feel they will surround themselves with people who leave little to chance. Unless, of course, M wishes to be found, or to lead me elsewhere.'

Just as my friend finished speaking, there came a strange noise on the still night air, a kind of pattering sound. It seemed to be coming from above. Holmes had heard it, too, and instinctively we looked up, just in time to see something descend from the roof. It came down at speed and, before we had a chance to move, it landed upon us. It was thick netting, of the sort used by fishermen. Both Holmes and I became entangled in it. As we struggled, we saw three figures leap down from the low roof who advanced on us.

'Your revolver, Watson,' cried Holmes as he withdrew his own and fired at the shifting silhouettes. I did the same. These shots halted their advance. Holmes fired again and this time there was a yelp of pain from the darkness and one of the figures staggered backwards. Holmes had obviously wounded the fellow.

Instinctively all three men retreated. 'Time to fly,' cried one. 'The point has been made, eh, Mr Holmes? Watch your back.' As these words echoed in the silence of the night, the three figures disappeared, blending into the darkness.

We struggled for some time to extricate ourselves from the netting.

'Well, that was a close call,' I said, dusting myself down.

'Not really,' observed Holmes, shaking his head. 'I am sure there was no danger. At times like this I am invincible.'

'I beg your pardon,' I stuttered, utterly taken aback by this statement.

Holmes smiled at my bewilderment. 'It is simply the case that M wanted to show me that I was never quite safe, that he has his eye on me at all times. It's just one of his tactics to unnerve me. He certainly wasn't going to let three of his bruisers kill me. He needs to do that himself in due course. It is not yet the time. He needs to play with me further.'

'You seem so very sure about this.'

'As sure as I can be under these rather bizarre circumstances. As far as I can recall I have never been involved in a mystery where I was the focus of the crime and my antagonist was unknown to me. It is exciting, challenging… and somewhat dangerous.'

Chapter Eleven

From the journal of John H. Watson

It was after midnight when we returned to Baker Street. Holmes had made quick work of the lock to Sullivan's Warehouse and, as he had surmised, the three men had left little evidence which would lead us elsewhere. They had evidently broken in, just as we had, and had spent limited time in the place, which had lain vacant for many months, judging by the dust and the weathered signs outside which advertised that the premises were to let. Traces of the three men were visible in just one office, which had been swept hurriedly, and Holmes measured incomplete footprints and marks which were invisible to my eyes, but which he confirmed matched those of the three individuals we had seen earlier that night. 'I will have one of my agents check the letting firm in the morning, but I think it is obvious that they have left no official trail in that area,' he said on leaving the cab.

I was none the wiser about this case than I was when we set out. As we made our way up the staircase, I was suddenly reminded of the two bodies we had left lying in our sitting room. Had Lestrade managed to remove them or were they still there waiting for us?

On entering, I was delighted to see that there was no sign of the two dead men or even the old trunk. However, there was another presence in the room. Lying prone on our chaise longue was the sleeping figure of our friend from Scotland Yard, Inspector Lestrade. His thin cheeks puffed gently as he let out a series of gentle snores.

Holmes and I exchanged smiles as we gazed at our sleeping beauty. Holmes stepped towards the hearth and rattled the coal bucket, extracting two large pieces with which he replenished the fading fire. The noise roused Lestrade from his slumbers and he sat up with a jerk.

'Ah, so you're back.'

'It would seem so,' said Holmes urbanely. 'Watson and I were about to have a brandy night cap. I trust you will join us.'

'I certainly will, gentlemen. It has been a long day – thanks to you.'

'Watson, if you will do the honours,' said Holmes slipping on his mouse-coloured dressing gown.

'So, what's it all about, Mr Holmes? Two dead 'uns in your rooms. It's a bit extreme, even for you. I need to know all the details so I can take the appropriate action. Who are the blighters? How did they die and how did they end up here?'

Holmes sighed and sipped his brandy before replying. 'It's not an easy tale to tell…'

'But it's one you will have to tell. You have involved an officer of the law in your activities and I must be fully cognisant of all the facts. You don't think I'd act as body removal man for any Tom, Dick or Harry. I did it as favour to you. I knew there would be a good and rational explanation and now I'm ready to hear it.'

'Of course,' said Holmes. 'Please be assured that I am most grateful for your assistance in this matter and I will put you in the picture as much as I'm able.'

In a methodical fashion, my friend recounted all the events that had occurred since we had been visited by the woman calling herself Elizabeth Courtney. Lestrade's face grew more bewildered and his frown deepened as Holmes continued his narrative. Holmes concluded, bringing the tale up to date with our visit to Sullivan's warehouse earlier that evening.

'There you have it, friend Lestrade. A pretty little puzzle, is it not?'

The inspector, who had been making notes during my friend's recital, sat back, snapping the book shut. 'Blimey, Mr Holmes, it makes no sense to me at all. So you think that our old comrade, Colonel Moran, is behind all this jiggery pokery?'

'I am convinced that he is involved. I will reserve my judgement for the moment as to whether he is the main mover and shaker, the mastermind behind it all.'

'Well, you realise that with two dead bodies involved, the matter is no longer just personal to you. It is now a police matter.'

Holmes contracted his brow and pursed his lips. He knew what Lestrade said was true but was unhappy at the prospect of sharing his investigations with the official police – or with anyone if it came to that. After a pause, he inclined his head in a gentle nod. 'I accept what you say, Lestrade, but you must understand also that I am a free agent and am not bound by rules and regulations imposed by Scotland Yard.'

'I understand that, Mr Holmes. No rules and regulations, indeed, but obligations to assist us in apprehending the murderer or murderers of the two men found dead on the floor of your sitting room.'

Holmes said nothing but shot me a cold glance, communicating his chagrin at this situation. He knew that to some extent he had to comply with the policeman's demands.

'Now, as I understand it,' said Lestrade, with a formal pomposity, 'one of the men was an actor playing the part of a police inspector. And the other was possibly a fellow called...' He referred to his notes. '... an Arthur Courtney.'

'Yes.'

'You say that the woman who came to ask for your help regarding her brother, this Arthur Courtney, actually gave you an address where the two of them lived.'

'Yes.'

'Well, it would seem that the first course of action would be to visit this address to see if there is any vestige of truth in her story.'

'I have already been there and drawn a blank,' I said.

'Have you, doctor? And what kind of blank is that?'

I told him of my visit to Ashtree House, my observation of the premises and my encounter with the neighbour and the information he gave me.

'Mmm, it may well be that you were told some kind of fairy story to put you off the scent. Couldn't it have been one of Moran's men placed there to mislead you?'

Before I had a chance to reply, Holmes leaned forward in his chair 'I think you may have something there, Lestrade. It is quite possible that an enemy agent was on guard waiting for me or one of my representatives to appear, in order to spin a cock and bull story designed to send me off in other directions. In fact, the more I think about it, the more I am sure you are right.'

This suggestion seemed preposterous to me, but I kept my own counsel.

Lestrade's eyes flashed with excitement at Holmes' statement. 'Right you are, Mr Holmes. There's our starting point. I think we should pay a call at Ashtree House tomorrow morning.'

Holmes shook his head. 'I think it would be very unwise for me to accompany you. They have already deflected my efforts with Watson, whom they will know is my associate. I think it would be more productive if you and another officer made this investigation and reported to me later in the day. I feel that you will discover more important information without my presence.'

Lestrade considered this notion for a moment before responding. 'You could be right, I suppose,' he said at length. 'And I am a representative of the official police, the law, not a private snooper, if you'll pardon the phrase. I do have powers that you do not possess.'

'Indeed you do,' said Holmes with a slight smile. 'You might also follow up this,' he said handing the policeman the ebony box containing the scorpion. 'I believe it to be a cheap item, manufactured in large numbers for the European market, and the scorpion a common species, no doubt procured from one of those establishments specialising in oriental curiosities. Perhaps your men may have some luck pursuing it with experts at the British Museum, while you make your presence felt in Chiswick?'

With a sudden movement, Lestrade rose from his chair. 'Excellent, Mr Holmes. That's what I'll do. I'll turn up in Chiswick in the morning with Sergeant Grey and see what's what. I feel certain I'll collect more information than Dr Watson was able to scoop up – no offence, Doctor.'

I smiled.

Slapping his hat upon his head, Lestrade moved to leave. 'I will report my findings in due course,' he said as a parting shot before closing the door behind him.

We waited until we heard heavy footsteps descending down the stairs before we allowed ourselves a little chuckle.

'I presume you have sent our friend on something of a wild goose chase,' I said. 'You had one of your fellows check with the estate agents whether the property really was on the market at the time. And the Irregulars confirmed that the gentleman I spoke to was a genuine neighbour. Wasting police time, Holmes?'

Holmes beamed. 'Lestrade is at his most enthusiastic and officious when he believes he has got the better of me. I only prompted him to follow his own nose, which we know from experience usually leads him in the wrong direction. I certainly wasn't about to let him hang on my coat tails while I try to unravel this mystery.'

'And the box?'

'Exactly as I stated – commonplace and untraceable. I should like to see the faces of the team at the British Museum when they present their artefacts for an opinion.'

'But what on earth do you do next?'

He leaned forward and picked up an object from the corner of his chemical bench and held it aloft like a magician producing a rabbit from a hat. I saw that it was the photograph of Arthur Courtney.

'How is that going to help?' I asked somewhat bemused.

'This is definitely the likeness of the murdered man who was delivered to us in a wooden trunk earlier today, viz Arthur Courtney; so then, we must pay a visit to the photographic studio where this picture was taken. Surely they will have records of their sitters and their addresses.'

'Of course. Why didn't I think of that?'

Holmes raised an eyebrow but did not respond. Instead, he examined the back of the photograph and stated, 'In the morning we will visit the photographic studios, Royal Images on Oxford Street, and make further enquiries regarding the dearly departed Mr Arthur Courtney.' Holmes rose from his chair and stretched. 'It has been a long weary day, Watson. Time for good fellows like ourselves to be heading for bed. A restful night's sleep is a must, for I fear we will have a similar eventful day on the morrow.'

Chapter Twelve

The woman sat in the candlelit gloom smoking a black cheroot. Colonel Sebastian Moran was seated on the other side of the desk. He was also smoking a small cigar and wondering why she so enjoyed sitting in such diffuse lighting. It was as though she wished to merge with the shadows, feeling at ease in the inky blackness. Her long pale face framed by her dark hair almost seemed to be floating in the darkness like a ghost.

'We have confused him somewhat,' she was saying in soft, precise and unemotional tones. 'But not confused him enough. He is much sharper and stronger than I thought. I can see now that it is time to stop playing with him – to turn the screw as it were. I trust all the final plans are in place to be instigated as soon as I give the order.'

'Yes,' said the Colonel. 'All we need is your word and the operation will begin.'

She gave a sigh of pleasure. It resembled the purr of a satisfied cat. 'Excellent. We know the fellow's set routine. As Doctor Watson reported, "he has his rails and he runs on them." Therefore it would seem that tomorrow evening around six o'clock would be an ideal moment to strike.'

'As you wish.'

'Oh, yes, Colonel, I do wish. It is my dearest wish.'

Chapter Thirteen

From the journal of John H. Watson

Despite the lateness of the hour when we retired, Holmes and I rose early the next morning, breakfasted quickly and we were in a cab heading for Oxford Street just after nine o'clock. 'It's such a fine morning, I suppose we could have walked, but just at the moment I wish to restrict my exposure on the street to a minimum,' he said, staring out of the cab window as though he might spot a would-be assassin at any moment.

'Airguns?' I queried.

'Yes. I am reminded of that actor fellow, Stead, how easily he was picked off.'

An image of that dark clean wound in the forehead of the false inspector came back to me and I gave a little shudder.

'Should we call on Lestrade for some police support to protect you?' I asked.

Holmes gave a grim smile. 'I fear that Scotland Yard's finest would be of little help in facing our current antagonist. The awful truth is, Watson, that at the moment I am not safe anywhere and I'm afraid, old chap, that may well apply to you also.'

'A cheerful thought.'

'I have been thinking that it might be propitious if you left London for a time. Have a holiday in the country somewhere perhaps, until this whole affair is over. I am very conscious that by being at my side you are placing yourself in great danger. This is my burden, not yours. It is somewhat reckless to place yourself at such risk.'

'Nonsense, Holmes. I have no intention of deserting you now. For three long years I wished that I could accompany you on some dangerous mission, believing that such an event would never happen again. Now you have returned, I am with you to the end.'

Holmes did not reply to my impassioned speech; he just gave me a knowing look. I could see from his taut features that he had been touched by my declaration.

The entrance to Royal Images did not match the grandeur of its name. It was a nondescript door on the corner of Oxford Street and Portman Street, at the far end of the thoroughfare near Tottenham Court Road.

As we entered, a little bell above the door tinkled, announcing our arrival. We found ourselves in a small room, the walls of which were adorned with a series of photographic portraits. All the eyes of the sitters, it seemed to me, were trained on us. Beyond a small counter there was a red velvet curtain, through which appeared a dapper wiry-framed man with a neatly trimmed grey beard. He flapped open the curtains in a dramatic fashion and then gave us a curt bow, his eyes sparkling brightly. 'Good day, gentlemen,' he said in a voice tinged with a French accent. 'I am Gustave Jourdan, the proprietor of this establishment but more importantly, the photographer supreme. I can assure you that you have come to the best studio in London.'

We both smiled and nodded in response.

'Now then, gentlemen, you are here because you wish to be photographed. I can assure you it is a painless, indeed a pleasant experience which will capture your likenesses for all time. Tell me, do you wish to be taken together or individually? Or perhaps both? Two such good-looking gentlemen would make a fine double shot.'

Before I could reject this suggestion with some force, Holmes held up a gloved hand. 'I am afraid we do not wish to be photographed.'

This statement brought puzzlement and dismay to the neat features of Monsieur Jourdan.

'I do not understand. I offer no other services. Your reply is most confusing.'

'We are in search of information.' Holmes withdrew the photograph from his pocket and presented it to Monsieur Jordan. 'This, I believe, is one of your portraits.'

The little man took the photograph and studied it. 'Ah, yes, it is one of mine: the studio monogram indicates as much.' He studied the picture more closely. 'I take many photographs and with so many faces sitting before my lens it is difficult to remember them once the photographs have been printed and taken away. But this gentleman... ah, yes, I remember him clearly. Arthur Courtney. That awful blemish on his face. It was a disfigurement most profound. My heart welled up with sympathy for the fellow. He asked me if I could treat the final print to reduce the effect of the mark on his features. I tried, as perhaps you can determine from the picture, but I could not eradicate it completely.'

'Having met the man, I can see that you have achieved a minor miracle,' said Holmes.

The photographer gave another brief bow. 'I like to think of myself as an artist. Although there are scientific aspects to the practice of photography, I also consider it as an art form, and one day I believe it will be recognised as such and be placed on a par with the work of the great water colourists and oil painters.'

'I am sure you are right,' agreed Holmes expansively.

Monsieur Jourdan returned his attention to the portrait of Arthur Courtney. 'However, I remain somewhat perplexed as to why you visit me.'

'We are desperate to contact Mr Courtney concerning a matter of great urgency and I was hoping that you could provide details of his home address.'

The photographer frowned. 'But you said you had met him.'

'Indeed, some time ago, but I am not in possession of such information. Now it becomes imperative that we contact him. It is a matter of life and death.'

Monsieur Jordan raised his eyebrows. 'Life and death, you say?'

Holmes gave an affirmative nod. 'I am afraid that I am not at liberty to divulge any details concerning the matter, but it will be of great assistance not only to me but to Mr Courtney himself if you can provide me with the information I require.'

'Who are you? Are you the police?'

'No. I am Sherlock Holmes.'

The photographer gasped. 'The detective…?'

'Yes.'

'Of course, I have heard of you. You are quite famous. This is in connection with a case, then?'

'Vital to it,' said Holmes in dramatic low tones.

'Very well. I understand. Of course, in that case I am happy to assist you in your work. Let me consult my ledger.' The little Frenchman made his way behind the counter and produced a large leather-bound book from the shelf beneath. He consulted the tome for some moments, muttering to himself as he turned the pages. Once or twice he stopped and peered more closely at the page in question before moving on. Eventually, he gave a cry of pleasure. 'Ah, here we are. I have it. Mr Arthur Courtney, September 1891. Three years ago. See, there is his address: Heaton Villa, King Charles Road, Clapham.'

Holmes jotted down the address on his cuff. 'Wonderful,' he cried. 'You have been of the greatest assistance, Monsieur Jourdan. I thank you most heartily.'

'It was of little consequence, but could I beg a favour of you in return. May I take your photograph? I must admit that a portrait of you in my studio would be a most impressive addition.'

Holmes smiled. 'I thank you for the compliment, but I fear I must decline your offer. I am very keen to remain as physically anonymous as possible. It is not appropriate for someone in my profession to be easily recognised. I trust you understand.'

'I suppose so,' the photographer admitted with some degree of disappointment.

'I expect that now we're taking a cab to Clapham,' I said once we were back on Oxford Street.

'How right you are, Watson. Let us see what clues the homestead of the late Mr Arthur Courtney can provide.'

Chapter Fourteen

The previous evening, just as dusk was falling over London, Mycroft Holmes was savouring a brandy and soda. He was sitting in the main members' chamber of the Diogenes Club and focused his gaze on the ornamental ceiling while his mind ranged over the various matters of state he would have to deal with when he returned to his office the following day. So sharp was his intellect that he was able to compartmentalise each item of business and consider the various issues involved individually. Problems were untangled, solutions to difficulties were mooted and irritations were smoothed away. Such cognitive activity did not lessen his enjoyment of his drink or the sense of ease that seeped gently into his broad frame as he lounged in the large leather armchair near the fire. There were only a few other members present at this early hour, most of whom Mycroft knew, but because of the nature of the club he did not acknowledge them. This, after all, was an establishment for the most unclubbable men in London. Social interaction was verboten. Within these walls each man was an island and was pleased to be so.

As he was draining his glass, one of the servants approached him and held out a silver tray, which contained a sheet of the club's notepaper. Mycroft took it and read the message it contained:

'A visitor to see Mr Mycroft Holmes in reception. He states that the matter is most urgent.'

Mycroft gave a nod to the lackey and with a sigh hauled his considerable girth out of the chair and with a ponderous gait made his way from the room. Passing into the narrow corridor that led to the reception hall, he did not notice two shadowy figures lurking in the gloom. One of them gave a deliberate cough, catching Mycroft's attention. As he turned, the other man slipped behind him. Mycroft felt a sharp prick on his neck.

'What the devil!' he cried. He had meant to say more but found that his tongue failed to respond. It lay dry and idle in his mouth. Equally, his knees suddenly lost their power to support him and he found himself sinking to the ground. As he did so, his vision blurred just before a grey cloud engulfed him and he slipped into partial unconsciousness.

Douglas Keating, the receptionist at the Diogenes, was, as usual, reading a novel as he sat at his post at the desk when he was distracted by a sudden noise in the foyer. Sudden noises were alien in the club. Looking up, with some surprise, he saw two men whom he did not know, holding between them a third man who appeared to be groggy to the point of unconsciousness. Keating recognised him as Mycroft Holmes, a founder member who was almost a part of the furniture.

'What on earth is going on, gentlemen?' asked Keating in the required hushed tones.

'Mr Holmes has had some sort of seizure,' said one of the men, a swarthy fellow with curly hair and large beetling eyebrows. 'We're taking him to a medical friend of ours around the corner to help sort him out. Closer than the hospital.'

'A seizure?'

'Yes, probably something to do with his blood pressure, no doubt. You knew that Mr Holmes suffered with high blood pressure.'

Keating shook his head. He was more concerned as who these two strangers were. He had never seen them before and they certainly didn't look like the calibre of gentlemen who usually frequented these premises.

'Mustn't dawdle, eh?' said one confidently. 'Got to get the old boy sorted out.'

Without further intercourse, the two men supported the inanimate form of Mycroft Holmes to the door of the club and out into the night.

Keating stared after them. He was not only puzzled by the incident but worried, too. It seemed so strange. The more he thought about it the more concerned he grew. As an avid reader of sensational novels, within seconds he had constructed a scenario in which the two men were neither members nor guests. He had, in essence, not noticed them enter and they had absconded with one of the most important members of the club. He felt he should inform someone but then the thought struck him that if he did say something, he may well be accused of dereliction of duty by allowing those fellows to enter unseen and then whisk Mr Holmes away without being challenged. It could be a sackable offence. An icy finger of fear ran up his spine. This notion certainly gave him pause for thought. Surely his imagination was charting conspiracy where none existed. A man of Mr Holmes's girth was quite likely to be stricken with some sudden illness. The gentlemen had probably entered the club when he had taken a quick break, or been here for some time, before he began his shift. No, he reasoned with himself, it would be best to say nothing, even to deny that the incident ever happened, should he be questioned. After all, the only person who may well complain would be Mr Mycroft Holmes himself and he was oblivious to what was happening. There was no one else in the foyer at the time. Yes, he must say nothing. With this resolution fixed firmly in mind, he returned to his novel, seeking, not with complete success, to divert himself with a fictional mystery.

Meanwhile, Mycroft Holmes, now fully unconscious, was sandwiched between his two abductors in a gloomy cab as it rattled through the darkened streets of the city. The two men were swigging whisky from silver flasks and chuckling heartily.

Chapter Fifteen

From the journal of John H. Watson

After leaving the Royal Images photographic studio, we made our way up to Oxford Circus and hailed a cab. Holmes checked the address he had written on his cuff and gave instructions to the cabbie. As we began our journey to Clapham, I asked Holmes what he was expecting to find there.

'I have considered several possibilities, one or none of which may be correct. We know that Arthur Courtney is dead – recently murdered – so we may well find an empty house. If that is the case, I trust we shall discover some clue, something that will help to lead us to those who killed him.'

'And why they killed him?' I added.

'Well, I think we know why: merely to use as a pawn in this treacherous game of cat and mouse that Moran and his colleagues are playing.'

'Great heavens! You mean to say there was no motive other than to provide a puzzling scenario designed to confound you?'

Holmes nodded sternly. 'That is how I read the riddle. It is very likely that he was chosen at random with no real connection with the perpetrators.'

'That is most shocking. An innocent man...'

'We are dealing with cruel, heartless individuals.'

'And the sister... Miss Courtney?'

'Most likely an invention. Obviously she wasn't the creature that visited us in our rooms.'

'Indeed, you demonstrated the truth of that. Is it possible that she was just an actress used by Moran to lure you into the game?

Holmes smiled. 'She undoubtably had dramatic skills, but she was no hireling. I am convinced that she is a major player in this dark business, a confederate of Moran.'

With these words, my friend lapsed into silence.

Heaton Villa was a compact Georgian dwelling situated in a quiet road not far from Clapham Common. Holmes paid the cabbie and we stood gazing at the property for some moments. All seemed quiet and normal, but there was no sign of life. At length we made our way up the path and rang the bell. We heard its shrill clang resonating in the interior of the building. We waited a while in silence but there was no response. On impulse, Holmes turned the door handle and remarkably it swung open with ease.

We exchanged glances: mine was one of surprise but Holmes wore an expression that suggested that he had anticipated this outcome. 'We are expected,' he said quietly. 'Take hold of your revolver, old friend. You may well need it.'

With some stealth we entered the house and stood in the hallway, listening for any discernible noise. There was none, not even the ticking of a clock. Holmes placed his finger to his lips and then beckoned me to follow him down the hall into the room on the right, which I took to be the sitting room. It was a drearily furnished chamber with tired furniture. The thin layer of dust lying on all the flat surfaces and the withered palm by the window clearly indicated that the room had not been attended to for a long while. But there was one surprising feature that caused my heart to skip a beat. Close to the chaise longue in the centre of the room was a small table upon which was a tall brass candlestick. The candle it was holding was still burning. It was now merely a stump, but it was clear to me that it must have been lighted within the last two to three hours. It had been lit for us. It was as Holmes had predicted: we had been expected.

'How did they know you would come here?' I asked.

'The photograph,' he snapped impatiently. 'They knew I would use it to obtain this address eventually. Their timing is impeccable – they must have eyes everywhere.'

As we moved further into the room, I observed that close to the candlestick was a bright shiny object and an envelope. Without a word Holmes rushed forward and snatched up the object. I could see that it was a gold watch. As my friend examined it, he gave out a groan and his shoulders slumped.

'What is it?' I asked.

He turned to me, his face drained and ashen. 'It is my brother's. It is Mycroft's gold watch.' He snapped open the casing and held out the timepiece. I could see the name 'Mycroft Holmes' inscribed there. 'It was given to him by Father on the occasion of his graduation from University.'

Holmes pocketed the watch. Picking up the envelope he extracted a sheet of paper. He read out loud the message it contained.

'"We have him, Sherlock. Since last night your brother has been in our keeping; although we cannot assure you that it is safe keeping. You have until midnight tomorrow to find him. If you do not, we shall feel obliged to cut his throat. Good luck. Moriarty."'

Holmes threw down the sheet of paper in frustrated anger.

'Moriarty! It cannot be. The devil is taunting me from the grave.'

I was at a loss what to say or do. I knew that a mixture of strong emotions must be swirling in Holmes' mind. He was no doubt angry that our opponents had yet again got the better of us, as though they had an invisible eye watching our every movement. Holmes was being played with and taunted, an alien state of affairs for my friend, which would be demoralising for him. He was invariably one step ahead of the enemy. Not this time. Also, there was the threat to his brother's life. Mycroft's fate had been left in his hands. The situation seemed to me an almost impossible one.

'Perhaps it is a bluff. Someone has stolen Mycroft's watch,' I said.

Holmes shook his head. 'This Moriarty individual – whoever he is – does not deal in bluffs. No, Watson, I am convinced that what the note says is true.'

'So what do we do?'

'Give me a moment to cudgel my brains. These fiends have left us no clues whatsoever as to where they have incarcerated my brother. I am like a blind man in uncharted territory.'

My heart sank at these words. Never had I heard Holmes express himself in such a negative fashion.

'Of course, old fellow,' I said in muted tones.

After a long pause, he retrieved the note, and pocketed it. 'There is a telegraph office two streets away from here. They have a telephone. We will establish whether Mycroft has been present at Whitehall today before trying the Diogenes Club.'

We made haste to the office, from where he made a quick telephone call to Mycroft's office and spoke to his assistant. I could see from Holmes' expression that he had received bad news.

'Mycroft has not been to his office today. That suggests that he was apprehended last night; therefore, the first port of call is the Diogenes Club. If he was taken from anywhere, it would be at the club. He has private quarters there. As you know his standard route is from there to his government office in the morning and returning in the evening as though the route were on rails. We will pick up the trail there.'

I nodded. I learned of this routine during the affair of the Greek interpreter.

Holmes gave me a grim smile. 'When there is no bread on the table, one has to rely on crumbs, though unlike Hansel, I doubt that the trail is assisting us, only leading us further into the forest.'

The Diogenes Club was situated down from the St James' end of Pall Mall, a short distance from the Carlton. We arrived there some forty minutes later. Holmes had been silent on the journey, his brow contracted in deep thought. I knew better than to break his concentration with simple chatter. We entered the discreet doorway and found ourselves in the well-appointed foyer. A fellow I recognised from my previous visits was situated behind the reception desk, reading a book. Holmes, who apparently knew the man by name, addressed him.

'Ah, Keating, you will remember me, Sherlock Holmes...'

'Why yes, sir.' He seemed nervous and a little alarmed to see my friend.

'I am looking for my brother, Mr Mycroft Holmes. I know it is rare for him to be at these premises during the day, but I wonder if you have seen him today – maybe at breakfast time.'

At the mention of Mycroft's name, Keating's features paled. There was a pause before he replied. 'He's ill, I'm afraid, sir.'

'Ill? What do you mean?'

'He was taken poorly in the club last evening. Two gentlemen, friends of his I assumed, carried him out in search of medical attention.'

Holmes gave me a swift glance. 'Really,' he said tartly, turning back to Keating, who seemed most uncomfortable with this conversation. 'Tell me exactly what happened.'

'All I know is that the two gentlemen told me that Mr Mycroft had had some kind of seizure connected with his blood pressure and they were taking him away for medical assistance.'

'Did any other member witness this "seizure"?'

Keating shook his head. 'None that I know of.'

'Who were these two men?'

Keating paused, his face registering great discomfort. 'I don't know,' he said at length. 'I cannot recall having seen them in the club before, although of course I don't know every member.'

'At what time was this?'

Keating screwed up his face as he attempted to recollect the moment. 'Sometime between six and seven o'clock, I reckon.'

'And I suppose their names do not appear in the register?'

Keating hesitated for a moment. 'I'm afraid I didn't see them arrive, sir, and when they left I checked the register but there were only a few guests that day and I know them all by sight.'

'And you didn't think it fit to report this incident?' snapped Holmes, his anger growing.

'Well, no. They said…'

'You are an incompetent fool!'

'I didn't think...'

'That sums up the situation accurately. What did these men look like? Can you describe them?'

At this request Keating's unease grew even more. 'They were just ordinary gentlemen. Tallish. Middle-aged, I'd guess. I'm afraid I didn't really take much notice,' he replied in querulous tones.

Holmes gave an exclamation of disgust.

'Oh, I remember that one of the men had black curly hair and very thick eyebrows.'

'Is that all?'

Keating gave a timid nod.

'Come, Watson, we have learned as much as we can here – which is virtually nothing.' He turned to Keating once more, his face still taut with fury. 'You are a disgrace to your calling, and have obviously learned little from those detective novels you are so fond of reading,' he snapped, before heading for the door.

We stood for a time on the steps of the Diogenes Club while Holmes brought his temper under control. 'That man should be removed from his post. He is not fit to be the gatekeeper of this or any other establishment,' he seethed.

'At least we did learn that Mycroft was escorted from here last night.'

'Yes, you are right, Watson, but not so much escorted as kidnapped.'

Suddenly Holmes' eyes fixed themselves on something ahead of him. I followed his gaze; it was focused on the cab standing close to the entrance of the club. There was always a cab man waiting there in readiness to provide services for members. Holmes hurried forward to address the gnarled figure hunched up on the driving seat.

'Where to, guvnor?' he croaked, the voice emerging from a throat ravaged by excesses of alcohol, tobacco and too many raw nights out in the open.

Holmes waved aside the query. 'Were you on duty last evening between six and seven o'clock?' he asked with some urgency.

The cabbie shook his head. 'Nah, last night was my night off. That would be Horace. Cab 248. It's his night off tonight. Lucky blighter.'

'What is Horace's last name?'

The cabbie chucked. 'I'm not sure I remember. I just calls him old Horace. Hang on a minute though...' He stroked his chin and closed his eyes for a few seconds. 'That's it,' he cried at length. 'Yeah, it's Hardcastle. Horace Hardcastle. I remembered the HH.'

'Thank you, my man.'

'S'all right, guv'nor. Here I hope old Horace hasn't been up to no mischief.'

'On the contrary. Come, Watson, this good fellow is going to transport us to the cab depot. I need a chat with HH.'

At the offices of the cab depot, the clerk in charge confirmed that it was indeed Horace Hardcastle's night off. 'But,' he added with some ire, 'the devil didn't turn up for his morning shift today. He'll get the length of my tongue when he does make an appearance and I'll make certain his pay is docked. We can't run a service if drivers come in just when they fancy it.'

Holmes agreed in a sympathetic tone, adding, 'If I could trouble you for Mr Hardcastle's address...'

Within minutes we were in our cab again on our way 48 Audley Gardens, Kennington Park Gate, the abode of Horace Hardcastle, the absent cab driver.

'Why do you want to see this fellow, Holmes?' I asked as we rattled along.

'Don't you see? He may well have seen the two men leaving the Diogenes Club. In fact, if luck is on our side, they may have used his cab to transport them somewhere. He may have a vital clue as to where they are holding my brother.'

'If that is the case, why didn't the kidnappers have their own cab to carry Mycroft away? That would have provided them with more security.'

Holmes gave me a brief smile. 'By using their own cab it would have been nigh impossible for us to find it or discover their destination. Remember these villains are intent on luring us into their darkness. I believe that we are meant to discover where they took Mycroft. My worry is that Hardcastle's non-appearance on duty this morning may have sinister implications.'

Soon our cab was threading its way through a long succession of bleak streets and dreary byways. In one of the dingiest and dreariest our driver suddenly drew the horse to a standstill. 'That's Audley Court in there,' our driver said, pointing to a narrow slit in the line of red-coloured brickwork. 'I'll wait here while you come back if you'd like.'

The arrangement made, we proceeded to our destination. Audley Court was not an attractive locality. The narrow passage led us into a quadrangle paved with stone flags and lined with sordid dwellings. Not for the first time, I mused sadly on the contrasts and inequalities of this city. Within a short space of time and but a few miles, we had moved from the civilised affluence of the Diogenes Club to the impoverished slums of south London where the poor folk lived a grim hand-to-mouth existence.

We picked our way through lines of discoloured linen hanging there until we came to the door of number 48. Holmes knocked loudly and almost on the instant it was wrenched open by a scruffy, hard-faced woman who, I guessed, looked older than her years. She gazed in amazement at us, as though she was expecting someone else standing on her threshold. Taking in our city clothes, she gaped and took a step back. 'You ain't the police, are you?' she cried, wringing her hands in some distress.

'No, no, Mrs Hardcastle. We have just come seeking a word with your husband.'

This news seemed to ease the woman's concern. 'Oh,' she said and then after a pause added, 'Well, gentlemen, I'd like a word with the good-for-nothing, too.'

'He is not here, then?' I asked.

'No, he ain't. He's on the booze again. He came home last night pickled as a newt and when he found the energy to rouse himself this morning round about noon, he upped and went out, and that was the last I seen of him.'

'Have you any idea where he went?' asked Holmes.

The woman gave a bitter grin, exposing a row of rotten teeth. 'Oh, yes, I know where he'll be. You'll find him carousing in the Three Tuns in Norton Street.' She gave a sigh. 'I've been down there before but it does no good. Anyway, I've these to care for, until our Ethel comes round when I gets off to work.' She gestured behind her and smiled at the two small, bright-eyed children who picked at her skirts, and then pointed vaguely up the stairs. 'And there's his mother. Can't leave her. Bedridden, she is. God knows how he can afford to pour so much ale down his face. Usually he don't have enough money to get so drunk. It seems he's come into a bit of cash. Probably some poor soul dropped his wallet in Horace's cab. He hasn't the way with him to hand it in and hope for a reward or use the money sensibly. Is it that you've come about? He's not going to be in trouble, is he?'

'No, I just want to have a word with him.'

'Well, as I said, The Three Tuns is your best bet. If you see the old fool, tell him to come home before he's spent all the cash and bring some grub with him. We're starvin' here.'

As we made our way back to our waiting cab, Holmes mused, 'It is a salutary lesson to meet such individuals as Mrs Hardcastle and to see how some poor folk have to survive in this city of ours. We are privileged, Watson, to live such comfortable lives and to sleep in warm beds with full stomachs. There but for the grace of God...'

Our cabbie knew the location of The Three Tuns and delivered us there in under ten minutes. There were a few men standing by the entrance, drinking from pot mugs and smoking clay pipes. Holmes and I passed by them into the ale house and made our way to the bar. The room was full of drinkers, some sitting at tables, others ensconced in booths on the perimeter. They were mainly men, although there were a few women whose heavily rouged countenances and exposed décolletages suggested they were streetwalkers, taking a few drinks before their night's work. What struck me was the fact that despite the number of customers, there was little noise: no raucous laughs, not heated arguments – in fact very little conversation at all. Faces were gaunt, with dead eyes. I recognised something of that feeling from the bleak years after Mary's death.

'Sad folk using alcohol as a means of escaping the cruelties of life,' observed Holmes quietly, reading my mind.

'As you observed earlier in Audley Court, it is a world we are very lucky not to inhabit,' I murmured as the ruddy-faced, white-aproned barman approached us.

'What's it to be, gents?'

Holmes ordered two glasses of beer. When they were delivered and coins exchanged in payment, Holmes leaned over the bar conspiratorially. 'I'm looking for a friend of mine, cabman by trade, Horace Hardcastle.'

The barman beamed. 'I think the geezer has taken up residency. He was in here most of last night and from about noon today. He's usually a moderate toper but when he has a bit of cash...' He broke off to give a deep throated chuckle. 'He's over there in the far booth, but whether he's still conscious I couldn't say.'

We glanced over in the direction indicated by the landlord and observed a lean fellow in in shabby grey coat, slumped back against the wall. His face was in shadow and we could not tell whether his eyes were open or not.

Holmes thanked the landlord for the information and we made our way to the booth. Hardcastle's eyes were drooping but as we took seats opposite him, they shot open in surprise. They were bloodshot and bleary and vacant. He stared at us for some moments trying to bring us into focus.

'I's got company,' he muttered thickly.

'Good day to you, Mr Hardcastle,' said Holmes. 'I would offer to buy you a drink, but it appears that you have had more than enough.'

Hardcastle grinned idiotically. 'You can never have enough,' he said and then fell back in his seat and closed his eyes again.

Holmes shook his arm. 'No, no, sir, pray do not go to sleep just yet. I need some information from you.'

The eyes opened slowly. 'Information?'

'I am prepared to pay for it.' Holmes held up a sovereign.

Hardcastle made a feeble attempt to take hold of it but Holmes pulled his hand away. 'Information first.'

'What d'ya want t'know?'

'Where did you take the three gentlemen you picked up outside the Diogenes Club last evening? The ones that paid you so very handsomely for the journey.'

Hardcastle thought for a moment and then with a great effort he shook his head. 'Don't know what you're talking about.'

'Oh, yes you do,' snapped Holmes, his tone hardening. 'The three men, one of whom was unconscious, were passengers in your cab last night.'

'What if they were?'

'They paid you well for the journey, didn't they? Very well indeed. Enough to keep you in drink for some considerable time.'

Hardcastle grinned. 'Yes, yes, they paid me well,' He parroted the words before the eyelids wavered once more.

Holmes shook him again, more vigorously. 'Wake up! You can slip into your drunken slumbers when you have told me where you took the three men.'

'Oh, no,' said Hardcastle rallying somewhat. 'Can't tell you that.' He raised a wavering finger to his lips. 'It's a secret.'

'It's a secret that you will share with me or you'll be in trouble.'

'Trouble.'

'With the police.'

These words had a gentle sobering effect on Hardcastle. He pulled himself up in his seat and pushed his muddled features towards Holmes. 'I ain't done anything wrong. I'm an honest bloke.'

'The men who paid you to keep quiet are wanted by the authorities. They are notorious felons. If you keep their secret, you will be regarded as their accomplice and a stretch in prison beckons.'

'But all I did was my duty as a cab man, and I promised to keep the destination secret.'

'Then you'll have to break your promise if you wish to retain your liberty.' Holmes held up the sovereign close to Hardcastle's face again. 'All you have to do is tell me where you took the three men.'

The drunken man still hesitated, his eyes focused on the golden coin. The light of greed flamed in his bloodshot eyes. He ran his thick tongue around his lips before replying. 'If I tells you, promise you won't let on it were me who blabbed. They threatened awful things would happen if I did.'

Holmes gave the man a tight grin. 'Your secret will be safe with us.'

'Well,' he said, leaning even closer and lowering his voice, 'it was to Deptford they had me going. And would you believe it, was to a bleedin' church.'

'A church,' I said with some surprise.

'Yeah. St Bartolph's. It's one of those deserted ones. Y'know, the ones no one goes to any more.'

'Deconsecrated,' murmured Holmes but I could see from the man's expression that the word meant nothing to him.

'It was close to the river near Rowland's Dock.'

Holmes dropped the coin on the table into a small puddle of beer. 'Come, Watson, we have what we needed.'

He paused at the bar and spoke with the landlord.

'Do you have a boy who could take a letter to an address in Kennington?'

'Young Eric could do that.'

'Good. Here's something for your trouble and something for Eric.'

He placed two silver coins on the counter and, under cover of a briefly scribbled message, slid a crisp five-pound note into an envelope, which he sealed and addressed to Mrs Hardcastle.

'He must take a cab. Here is the fare. And he must see that this is delivered directly into her hands straight away.'

On returning to our own cab, Holmes addressed the driver. 'We have more work for you tonight, if you are up to it.'

The fellow grinned and touched his cap in a salute. 'Of course. If you're paying, I'm yours to command. Where to now?'

'Deptford. St Bartolph's church.'

Chapter Sixteen

A fter his conversation with the two gentlemen, Horace
Hardcastle had sobered up enough to buy himself another
pint. As he resumed his seat, he felt very pleased with himself.
He'd earned a bright shiny sovereign just for telling the two
gents where he took his passengers last night. A self-satisfied leer
spread across his face.

At a nearby table, a hawk-like individual had been keeping a
watchful eye on Hardcastle and had witnessed the interview with
the two men he knew to be Sherlock Holmes and Doctor Watson,
including the transaction involving a sovereign. His job here was over.
Things had gone according to plan. With a grin, he rose from his stool
and giving a slight nod to Hardcastle, he sauntered out of the bar.

Mycroft Holmes tried to clear his head of the fog that was
surrounding his brain. He was wondering quite where he was

and, more particularly, why he had been placed in this pleasant room. The leather armchair was comfortable, the table at his side contained a box of corona cigars, a decanter of whisky and a bowl of his favourite bon bons. His only discomfort was the set of manacles around his ankles and the tight belt around his ample waist, which secured him to the chair. From time to time a shadowy figure wearing a mask would enter the room to enquire if there was 'anything he desired'.

His response, 'My freedom,' was met with a polite chuckle before the masked figure withdrew.

What the devil, he thought, with suppressed desperation, was going on? He reasoned that there was no political motive behind this kidnapping. The international situation was quite stable at the moment; there were no imminent unpleasant incidents likely to stir up the fairly calm waters. The alternative proposition was something concerning... well, yes, Sherlock, of course. Whenever he was seriously inconvenienced, his brother was the cause. Some criminal involvement no doubt. At this thought, a spark of anger ignited briefly within his breast, but died away quickly. It was futile to be angry with his brother, although it was most likely that his imprisonment was concerned with one of Sherlock's investigations. He could not work out if he should be seriously worried by his kidnap and that he was in real personal danger, or if it was simply that he was just being used as a pawn in some nefarious game.

As he was pondering this dilemma, the door opened and a figure entered, but this time it was no longer the masked man but a woman, who wore no face covering. She was tall and thin, with a long face which bore sharp features. She moved slowly towards him, a gentle smile on her lips.

'I trust you are reasonably comfortable, Mr Holmes,' she said.

'Not really. I would much prefer to be elsewhere and unfettered,' he replied.

'Ah, you must be patient a while longer, but all will be well in the long run.'

'I am gratified to hear it. Perhaps you would be kind enough to tell me what all this is about.'

Her smile broadened. 'I am afraid I cannot do that, but in the fullness of time I am sure everything will become clear to you.'

'No doubt my brother Sherlock is involved...'

'Ah, the redoubtable Mr Sherlock Holmes, the famous detective... You are fond of him?'

'He is my brother. We rub along. Blood is a great coagulant. I would be most discomfited if he came to harm.'

The woman sighed. 'In that case, I should prepare yourself to be discomfited.'

It was early evening by the time Sherlock Holmes and Doctor Watson arrived at St Bartolph's in Deptford. The area where the church stood had once housed a thriving dockland community in the earlier part of the century, but now most of the houses were empty or derelict. The church which had served these people was also abandoned and in a state of disrepair. Some of the stained-glass windows had been shattered by vandals and broken drainpipes had encouraged the growth of moss and the spread of damp. The adjacent graveyard was an overgrown jungle.

Holmes and Watson alighted from the cab and stood for some time staring at the crumbling edifice, which was slowly turning to a grey silhouette against the darkening sky.

'I must go in there alone,' said Holmes softly.

'No,' cried Watson. 'I cannot allow it. We have come so far together...'

'I know how you feel, old fellow,' said Holmes taking his friend's arm, 'but I am convinced there is great danger waiting for me inside the church and I am not prepared to put the life of my dearest friend at risk by allowing him to accompany me. I need to tackle this situation on my own without worrying about the safety of a companion. That would only distract me. Believe me, it is for the best.'

Watson knew there was no point in arguing with Holmes over this matter. It was clear that he had made up his mind.

'As you wish,' he said with solemn reluctance.

'Fear not, Watson, I have my wits and my revolver. You know from experience that I can take care of myself.' Holmes turned and made his way towards the church. He passed through the wicket gate up the path towards the large oak door. He knew that if it was locked, this would be another barrier he would have to overcome, but he found that the large rusty ring turned easily and the door swung open with a gentle creak. To his mind, it was clear indication that once more he was expected.

Taking a deep breath, he made his way through the porch and into the narthex. Here he stood and took account of his bearings and the interior of the church. There was a tangible air of damp and decay in the atmosphere. As he gazed around he saw the signs of decay and rot. Dust hung like a fine curtain in the air and the stone walls were stained with water damage and mould. In the sepulchral gloom, Holmes could see that down the central aisle beyond the nave, there were several long candles burning on the raised chancel, creating an eerie shadowy glow around the altar as though in readiness for his arrival. As in the case of The Bar of

Gold and Arthur Courtney's house, he had been lured here.

Apart from a few birds fluttering up in the eaves, there was no sound. Holmes sensed that he was being watched, but there was no visual evidence that there were others in the church. He was tempted to call out his brother's name but thought better of it. If Mycroft were here, he would soon find out. He hoped that this was not just another wild goose chase.

Slipping his revolver from his overcoat pocket, he began to make his way down the nave towards the altar, past the rows of rotting pews. As he did do, he kept all his senses on full alert, moving his head from side to side in an effort to catch any movement in the shadows. There was none.

As he progressed slowly and cautiously down the central aisle, he observed that there was something – a dark shape – at the far end of the altar. He narrowed his eyes to focus on the silhouetted form. Was it moving or was it made to seem so by the shifting shadows created by the flickering candles? Holmes could not be sure. He tightened his grip on his revolver and continued forward. A few more feet and he could make out that the dark shape was in fact a body, secured to a heavy chair by thick rope. A black sack had been placed over the head, which lolled on its chest.

The body was not moving.

Then he heard a noise emanating from the back of the church. A strange crackling, scraping noise. He spun round and gazed hard into the gloom. He saw nothing and silence reigned once again.

Holding his breath, he waited for a repeat of the sound. There was none and so he turned his attention back to the figure on the chair. Was it Mycroft? If so, was he alive? Or was this the corpse of his brother? As Sherlock Holmes approached the chair, he felt his body tense and his heart rate increase as he reached out his hand to take hold of the sack covering the head and gently pulled it free. What he saw made him gasp and take a step backwards.

The body was a dummy – not a real person at all.

The head was some sort of papier mâché concoction and the face was just a flat piece of cardboard on which was written a message in capital letters:

'FOOLED AGAIN, SHERLOCK. GOODBYE, MR HOLMES.'

As he read these words, the ear-splitting boom of an explosion rent the air. Instantly there came the thunderous sound of falling masonry. It was clear to Holmes that some kind of explosive device had been triggered. The cacophony was accompanied by a cloud of dust which rose from the rear of the building. Great grey amorphous plumes billowed forth, rolling towards him. At the same time, to his dismay, Holmes saw flames rise up at the far end of the church. Fierce angry tongues of yellow stretched towards the roof. Within seconds a further blast occurred, nearer to the altar this time. With grinding groans, two of the church pillars snapped into several sections, thundering to the ground. Their demise brought part of the vaulted roof with it. Holmes gasped for air as the thick mist of choking dust enveloped him. Moving forward, he could see through the murk that the roaring flames were in the process of taking possession of the whole building. A third explosion followed very quickly. This time it came from behind the altar. A shower of glass splinters rained down on him from the high windows. The walls of the church began to shake violently and fold in amongst themselves.

The smoke and dust produced an atmosphere like a dense London fog. Hand clasped to his mouth, Holmes stumbled forward like a blind man. Desperately, he began to feel his way in the gloom, unsure which way to turn. A feeling of anger grew within his breast. 'By Heaven,' he thought, 'I have been fooled again and I've walked blithely into this death trap. They mean this church to be my final resting place.'

A fourth thunderous detonation from somewhere in the area of the vestry shook the ground beneath him. It signalled the final death warrant on the building. Its very structure began to disintegrate. Like a child's toy, the church surrendered to its own destruction. Stones and rafters cascaded down all around him as the walls crumbled and caved in. A piece of masonry struck him on the shoulder. With a cry of pain, he dropped to the ground, but with great determination he to dragged himself to his feet. As he did so, a falling rafter narrowly missed him. He staggered forward towards the vestry, clutching his shoulder, his stooping figure melting into the fog of smoke and dust.

Chapter Seventeen

A solitary carriage pulled up on Westminster Bridge. The door opened silently and a corpulent figure was ejected unceremoniously from the interior on to the pavement. 'There you go. Job done. Thank you for all your help, Mr Holmes,' sneered a voice from the interior, followed by a deep sarcastic laugh. In an instant the door was pulled shut and the cab drove away at speed, leaving the figure alone on the bridge as the midnight hour approached.

Mycroft Holmes staggered to the parapet, his mind still confused from the drugs they had injected him with. He gazed down at the dark waters flowing below him. A barge slipped by under the bridge and he tried to focus on the vessel while, at the same time, desperately attempting to clear his brain of the fog that surrounded it. For five minutes he leaned forward taking in large gulps of the cold night air.

One question thundered in his mind: 'What in Heaven's

name was that all about? Why had he been kidnapped and then released?' Slowly, as clarity of thinking returned, he knew the person who would most likely be able to answer those puzzling questions: his brother, of course.

Chapter Eighteen

From the journal of John H. Watson

I watched Sherlock Holmes enter the church and a strange feeling of dread filled my senses. On impulse I took one step forward with the intention of following him, despite his instructions to wait outside, but I held myself in check. I knew in my heart that his advice was always the best. He was, after all, the wisest man I knew. Despite my concern for his safety it would be foolish, and maybe dangerous for both of us, if I acted against his wishes. However, I had determined to follow him inside if he had not emerged within ten minutes.

And so, with great reluctance and dark apprehensions, I stood, waiting in the growing gloom of the evening, wondering what was happening inside St Bartolph's church. Then the silence of the night was shattered by a tremendous boom. The first explosion shook the front of the building. The porch vibrated violently before disintegrating in a shower of dust and a fusillade of splintered stone. For some moments I remained frozen to the spot with shock. By the time the second explosion occurred, I was clambering over the rubble in a desperate attempt to gain entry to the church. To my dismay, the doorway was blocked by a small mountain of debris and I was driven back by a thick cloud of sooty dust which began to choke me.

'Holmes!' I cried hoarsely, although I knew the call was futile. By the time the fourth explosion came, the whole place started to reverberate and collapse in on itself. It was if some giant invisible hand were shaking the structure in an act of violent destruction.

I gazed in horror as, in a shimmer of dust and flames, the church swiftly crumbled before my eyes. I ran around the perimeter of what was left of the building, looking for a doorway, an opening, anything, calling Holmes's name. I couldn't get close enough due to the fierce heat of the flames, which was burning my cheeks. There was no sign of my friend. Suddenly I felt a strong hand tugging on my shoulder.

Could it be? Was it Holmes?

Then I heard a voice. 'Come away, sir. You'll be killed if you don't.' It was the cab man who then grabbed my arm and pulled me away from the building, dragging me down the path and on to the road. I turned and stared back at the inferno that had once been a church. My senses were quite numb as I watched the dark clouds of smoke and tongues of fire billowing up into the evening sky. It was all over in minutes. This was how it ended.

'Holmes,' I muttered to myself, fully aware that my friend could not have survived such a disaster – a manmade disaster wrought by his enemies. I had a vision of him lying dead, sprawled on the floor of the church, his body trapped beneath a pile of masonry, and now consumed by fire. As this image flashed up in my imagination, I confess that I shed a tear. I had lost my friend three years ago and now it had happened again. For real this time.

'Are you all right, guv'nor?' asked the cab man.

I had no words of reply.

'I reckoned if your pal was in there, he's a dead 'un,' he said matter-of-factly. 'No one could have survived in there.'

I returned my gaze to the rubble and flames that had once been a place of worship. Indeed, the cabman was right: no one could have survived in there – not even Sherlock Holmes.

It was approaching midnight when I returned to Baker Street. I had been to Scotland Yard and reported what had happened that evening and the death of Sherlock Holmes. As it happened, I just caught Inspector Lestrade coming off duty and he took me into his office and gave me a brandy while offering his condolences. 'I'd just got used to having him around again,' he said mournfully, giving me an awkward pat on the shoulder. 'Never thought he'd go like that. Who d'you reckon set the trap?'

'I'm not sure. Moran is likely to be mixed up in the business but Holmes thought he wasn't the mastermind behind the things that have been occupying us for the last few days.' I gave Lestrade a brief outline of recent investigations.

'Blimey, it looks like they were really playing with Holmes, doesn't it? And you say they've got his brother now.'

I nodded. 'He was used as bait, I suspect. He may already be dead.'

Lestrade ran his fingers through his hair and sighed heavily. 'What a rum state of affairs. To lose two of the brightest fellows in London is a hell of a blow.'

'Of that I am well aware,' I said softly as a wave of sadness washed over me. I wished Lestrade goodnight and left the building quickly.

* * *

I walked from Scotland Yard back to Baker Street. I wanted fresh air and time to think and, if I am honest, to mourn a little. The enormity of the night's events was only just beginning to register fully in my mind. Sherlock Holmes was dead and I had no idea who was responsible for his demise. Mycroft Holmes had been kidnapped and it was more than likely that the villains would have done away with him. The world had gone mad and I was left behind, stranded without a clue as to what I was going to do now. I could not remember feeling as low and miserable as I did when I trudged up Baker Street towards 221B. Even at Reichenbach I knew who was involved and had satisfaction in the knowledge that the fiend had perished, too. There were no untidy loose ends then. But now…

With weary limbs I mounted the stairs to our rooms. As soon as I entered, I sensed that there was someone in there in the darkness. I reached for my revolver from my overcoat.

'Don't shoot, Watson,' said a familiar voice. 'I've endured enough violence for one night.'

I felt a little giddy for a moment. Could I believe my ears? Was my grief playing tricks on me? I reached out for the gas mantle and turned it up. There, sitting in his favourite chair was Sherlock Holmes. His clothes and hair were coated in a fine film of grey dust and his face was streaked with dirt and specks of blood. I gaped in speechless shock. 'Great Heavens,' I said at length finding my voice, 'I can't believe it! I am so happy to see you, but I… I just can't believe it. I thought you had perished in that church.'

Holmes gave me a gentle smile. 'I nearly did.'

'How… how on earth did you manage to escape?'

'Fortunately, I was able to run to the vestry as the whole structure of the building was falling about my ears. As luck would have it, the final explosion had blown a hole in a wall at the rear – a hole just big enough for me to crawl through. I managed to stagger away into the graveyard beyond before the whole place was reduced to rubble. It was then that I collapsed and lost consciousness for a short time. When I came to, I was underneath one of those table tombs, which was partially collapsed and had protected me from the heat and most of the debris. It was pitch black and the building itself was just a jagged shell, partly illuminated by the flames which were still caressing the ruins. It had attracted a small crowd of curious souls. It was possible that amongst them were the perpetrators of the destruction, my would-be murderers. They could have been admiring their handiwork or keeping an eye out to see if there was any sign of me. Keeping to the shadows, I slunk away and managed to make my way back here by the rear door. A glass of brandy and an ounce of shag tobacco and I soon began to feel like my old self again.'

'It is a miracle that you escaped,' I said.

'I wouldn't place the incident amongst such biblical proportions, but certainly the Fates smiled on me tonight. I knew there was danger waiting for me in St Bartolph's but I had not reckoned on explosions. I was aware that the whole scenario had been carefully orchestrated and that I was led to the church by the nose. However, I believed that it was going to be another blind alley. I was wrong. They had obviously decided it was time to bring down the curtain on their dark charade.' Holmes shook his head sadly. 'I misjudged the situation, I'm afraid.'

'I had not thought that Moran would play this sort of murderous game,' I said. 'As you have said, he is a hunter. He does not taunt his prey. He goes in quickly for the final kill.'

'You are quite right, Watson. Moran is obviously involved in this business but he is not the cunning leader of the pack, the one who has planned this or makes the decisions. It is as though the ghost of Moriarty has risen from the grave and has taken control of his old Organisation again, using Moran as in days of old as his trusty aide-de-camp.'

I shook my head. 'Don't even think such a thing. Moriarty is dead and he certainly cannot operate from the hereafter.'

Holmes gave me a thin smile. 'Don't worry, Watson, I am not going senile or subscribing to the Spiritualists' beliefs, but the whole structure of this persecution has the mark and feel of the Professor about it. I cannot shake that thought from my mind.'

I was about to respond to this when my friend sat forward in his chair and with an urgent gesture placed his forefinger to his lips to silence me. 'Listen,' he whispered fiercely.

I strained my ears and heard the heavy tread of erratic footsteps making their way up our stairs.

Holmes whipped his revolver from his pocket and then grabbed the poker from the hearth and handed it to me. 'Quick! Behind the door, Watson.'

I did as instructed and waited, weapon in hand. The footsteps stopped, the doorknob began to turn slowly and the door swung open. A burly figure stumbled into the room. 'Sanctuary,' a voice said in a melodramatic fashion.

'Mycroft!' cried Holmes leaping from his chair.

'Indeed, 'tis I. Well, there is nothing wrong with your eyesight, brother mine,' said Mycroft Holmes, staggering further into the room. 'Sanctuary – or at least a comfortable armchair and a brandy. I am somewhat fatigued. The last twenty-four hours or so have been quite demanding of my spirit and constitution.' He glanced at me. 'Oh, Dr Watson, you can come from behind the door with your sturdy weapon now. I mean you no ill.'

Holmes helped his older brother to a chair. Once seated there, Mycroft scrutinised his sibling, a relieved smile on his sharp features. 'Great Heavens,' he chortled, 'it is the Ghost of Christmas Past. I see that you, too, have had your travails.'

'Indeed, and I cannot tell you how delighted I am to see you in the flesh. I feared for your life, dear brother.'

Mycroft gave a dark chuckle. 'You were not alone in that concern. So, Sherlock, what is this all about? I knew the moment I was abducted from the Diogenes Club that you would in some way be involved in the matter.'

'First tell me of your adventures so that I can slot them into the dark jigsaw puzzle I am attempting to assemble.'

Mycroft shrugged his substantial shoulders. 'There is little to tell – some of which, no doubt you have deduced. I was sedated in the Diogenes Club by two fellows whose faces I never saw. One of the brutes stuck some sort of dart in my neck and I drifted off into dreamland in a matter of seconds. I woke from my drugged slumbers in a large, comfortably appointed room – comfortable apart from the fact that I was secured to a chair. I have no clear idea where I ended up but, on the return journey, when I was more *compos mentis* than the state I had been in on my arrival, I was able to make some deductions. The location is some twenty minutes from London, probably south of the city. It is a rural spot, as country silence, apart from the rustle of trees in the wind, the occasional owl and fresh night air indicated. A substantial pile situated in parkland. Jacobean. I was fed and wined and attended to by individuals who kept mainly to the shadows and wore masks. Interestingly, I was visited during my imprisonment by a woman.'

'Really?' Holmes suddenly grew alert and tense. 'What can you tell me about her?'

'She was an alluring creature. Not exactly beautiful, but with strong aquiline features. Tall and assertive. She had a voice that was tinged with a very slight accent. French, I should think, but she spoke excellent English. I am not very good at judging the ages of women, but I would say that she was in her late twenties or early thirties.'

'She sounds very much like my dubious client, Elizabeth Courtney. Although there was no trace of accent in her voice when she visited me, it is clear that she was an accomplished actress and adopted her delivery accordingly. And she seemed to be in control of this operation?'

'Difficult to say for certain. She was not present when the men were in the room, but she gave the impression of an authority which they did not possess.'

'Interesting. Very interesting. Do continue,' said Holmes, his features eager and tense.

'There is little more to say. Earlier this evening I heard a flurry of activity in the chamber beyond and then one of the masked men came in and without a word stuck another dart in my neck. This time the drug was not as powerful. I came to in a closed carriage rattling away with two of the felons by my side. They bundled me out of the carriage on Westminster Bridge and left me there. With some effort I made my way here in search of an explanation and some sustenance.' He raised his brandy glass. 'To be honest, Sherlock, the last twenty-four hours have seemed like some bizarre scenario created by Lewis Carroll. '

'I am very sorry that you were dragged into the matter. I had no idea that our enemy would involve you.'

'I was used, no doubt, in order for you to do something you were reluctant to do – something illegal perhaps. My survival was your spur.'

'Something of the sort,' said Holmes evasively.

'Well, Sherlock,' he said, giving him the sort of stern but indulgent stare that only an elder sibling could, 'seeing as I have undergone a series of indignities on your behalf, I think it only right and proper that you put me fully in the picture.'

'Indeed.' Holmes gave me a brief glance before launching into a full account of all the events that had occurred since the arrival of the fake client Elizabeth Courtney in our chambers until his remarkable escape from the explosions at St Bartolph's church. Holmes had a remarkable facility for relating the important facts of the scenario in a swift and concise manner. He dealt with all the pertinent details of the case with great economy.

Mycroft Holmes leaned forward in his chair, entranced by this recital. He sat in silence for some moments after Holmes had concluded his tale before responding. 'Fascinating,' he said at last. 'The crime here was to taunt and confuse you and then destroy you. It is obviously a revenge plot, a *vendetta* as the Sicilians would say. But revenge by whom? The good Professor Moriarty is out of the picture. Moran, as you say, would be much more direct in his attempt to eliminate you. It is as though someone was determined to establish their superiority before killing you.'

Holmes nodded vigorously. 'That is how I read the riddle – but for the life of me I cannot think of anyone who has such a cunning mind and a desperate desire to see me dead.'

'Well, I can hardly think it can be the young woman I saw, and yet...' said Mycroft.

'I second that "and yet",' said Holmes keenly, pursing his lips.

'Your description of her and your reference to a slight French accent makes me wonder... The name Madame Defarge was mentioned by Soapy Sanders.'

Mycroft nodded. 'I have heard of her, of course. A criminal lady operating in Paris some years ago. But I hardly see the connection.'

Holmes shrugged. 'Maybe there isn't one, or maybe it is hidden in the shadows. Could you contact your friends across the Channel, Mycroft, and find out more about this nefarious femme fatale? A photograph or some likeness would be of use. Also, could you delve into the Moriarty papers which I know you hold and see if you can come up with any direct connection with the Professor and France?'

Mycroft gave a mock salute. 'Of course. It shall be done. In the meantime, what do you intend to do?'

To my surprise, Holmes rubbed his hands with glee, a broad smile materialising on his tired and grubby face. 'Now? Well, as I am once again presumed dead, I am determined to remain so. It will place me in an ideal position to retaliate.'

Chapter Nineteen

❧

From the journal of John H. Watson

The funeral of Sherlock Holmes took place a week later. As soon as he had emerged from the devastation of St Bartolph's, Holmes had sent a message to Lestrade to instruct him to ensure that the church perimeter was secured and a 'body' was seen to be removed from the ruins. The funeral was a well-attended affair with a smattering of old, grateful clients come to pay their last respects to the man who had brought peace and security to their lives through his investigations. There was a contingent from Scotland Yard, including Inspectors Lestrade, Gregson, Hopkins and Patterson, plus a large press presence. The world had been shocked by the sudden death of 'the great detective' shortly after his return to London, having been thought dead for three years. The newspapers had not missed the irony of the situation. One of the gutter rags had even created a sordid cartoon showing Holmes carrying a candle walking into a mausoleum with the caption, 'I'm back!'.

The weather was appropriately gloomy for such a sad occasion. Dark clouds loured in the slate-grey heavens and a fine sheen of rain hung in the air. I chaperoned Mrs Hudson, unsteady on her feet and uncertain in her role as a grieving landlady. It was clear to me from her demeanour that she wished she had no part in this dark charade. Mycroft provided a stoical and dignified presence as the mourners made their way through the graveyard to the burial plot. As we progressed, I scanned their faces. I felt sure that someone from the enemy camp would be amongst them, here to gloat and draw the final line under the life of their nemesis. Of course, it was impossible to spot any possible culprit: evil can wear a placid and anonymous face.

However, I did notice in the shadows beneath a nearby elm tree the figure of a grave digger leaning on a shovel. He was a tall, spare individual with a goatee beard wearing wire-rimmed glasses. He wore a large woolly hat pulled well down over his forehead. I noticed that as the coffin was lowered into the grave a thin smile touched his lips. An observer at his own funeral.

Mycroft and I threw a handful of dirt onto the coffin, which echoed like distant rifle fire in the stillness of the graveyard. And then it was all over, and the mourners began to disperse. I noticed that the grave digger had disappeared. Mycroft shook my hand and hurried away. For a man who usually never showed his emotions he appeared surprisingly upset by the whole proceedings.

I helped Mrs Hudson into a carriage and was about to join her when I felt a hand on my shoulder. It was Lestrade. There was an unfortunate twinkle of amusement in his eyes. 'The second Holmes funeral, eh, Doctor?' in said quietly, digging me in the ribs. 'We must stop meeting like this.'

I said nothing but gave him a hard stare.

'No doubt we shall be seeing each other anon. You never know when the game will be afoot.' He gave a little wink and turned away.

I returned with Mrs Hudson to Baker Street and the empty sitting room waiting there.

Chapter Twenty

Later that day, in a small dark private office in one of the government buildings, Mycroft was in conference with a scruffy, bearded individual: his brother.

'As requested, I made discreet enquiries with my contact at the Sûreté in Paris regarding Madame Defarge. Indeed, she was a successful criminal operative, running a small but very efficient band of criminals a few years ago. Robbery, blackmail, murder for profit – that kind of thing. My contact assured me that she proved to be a very irritating thorn in their flesh at the time. And then she fell silent and a body, which was assumed to be hers, was washed up on the banks of the Seine at Île Saint-Germain, an island not far from the centre of the city. Her case is now closed with the Sûreté.'

'There is no photograph, no likeness?'

Mycroft shook his head. 'All that is known is that she is a fairly young woman, tall and slim with strong features. Possibly dark-haired, but she was a mistress of disguise.'

Holmes nodded. 'It could be the Courtney woman but then...' He sighed. 'All will be revealed in time. Any other news?'

'Indeed. I have a few nuggets of information, the result of my time burning the midnight oil poring over the Moriarty papers. Ah, the reams of private documents hidden away and unearthed after the Professor's infamous swimming lesson. What one man can secrete ingeniously, another can discover.' Mycroft chuckled to himself.

Holmes waited silently for his brother's revelations.

'It seems that Moriarty sent regular payments to an educational establishment in Paris from 1868 to 1878. And here is the really interesting part. It was a conservatoire for young ladies.'

The two brothers stared at each other for some moments, their features still but their eyes glittering with excitement.

'You are no doubt thinking what I am, Sherlock.'

'Of course. It could be that the muddy waters are growing clearer.'

'Quite.' Mycroft paused for a moment and then, with cool efficiency, he extracted a manilla file from the top drawer of his desk and pushed it in Holmes' direction. 'Now, to other matters. I have found the ideal man for you,' he added with a smirk of satisfaction.

Part Four

The Lion's Den

Chapter Twenty-one

Jacob Brooks lay back on his prison bunk and sighed. It was an expression of contentment. For him the world was getting sweeter by the day. He had at last got the cell to himself. The fetid old lag who had been his cell mate for twelve months – the one who snored when asleep and who had bored him rigid when awake – had gone. Now he had the place to himself and it smelt a great deal sweeter as a result. He had peace, quiet and time to contemplate his freedom – for it was coming soon. He only had two months to go in this hellhole before he was able to breathe the fresh air of liberty once more. Three years he'd been locked away, three years in which his hair had turned grey and his mind had begun to atrophy. This decay would soon end. He couldn't wait for those prison gates to open and for him to stroll – and, by God, he would stroll, nonchalantly as well – out into the streets of London.

The icing on his bun was the prospect of returning to his old profession – safecracker. He'd had a surprise visitation about a month ago. The Organisation was gradually reforming under a new leader and the old gang was being recruited. With his special talents, those skilful sensitive fingers, he had been informed that his services would be required. Was he interested? Of course, he was. It warmed his heart to receive the offer. It would be like the old days. In one sense he would miss the Professor but, in reality, he had seen little of the man himself; the cunning devil remained a shadowy figure for obvious reasons. However, he was a good boss and looked after his men. If they were loyal and useful, he kept them safe and well paid for efficient work.

Brooks sighed. If only he had a smoke to complete his contentment. Snout was like gold dust in this rat hole. Ah well, in two months he could have as many smokes and pots of ale as he wished. At this thought a gentle smile creased his grey features. This disappeared in an instant as he heard the grating noise of the key turning in the lock. What now? he thought as he pulled himself up in his bunk. The door swung open with force and crashed against the side wall. In the aperture stood a squat, burly prison officer, his uniform straining over a large stomach. This was Officer Buchanan. His large round red face was threaded with veins, the result of gluttony and drink, and the mean piggy eyes spoke of a vindictive nature.

'Top of the morning to you, Brooksey. I've brought you another playmate,' he said with cheerful malice. 'He's been moved here to serve out his penal holiday with us.' He gave a raw laugh and then stood aside and ushered in another prisoner – a tall, shaven-headed man with gaunt features, shifty eyes and a large bristling moustache. A curved scar adorned his right cheek and he had a straggly goatee beard sprouting from his narrow chin.

Jacob Brooks jumped off his bed and adopted an aggressive

stance. 'I don't want another cellmate, I want to be left alone.'

Buchanan laughed. 'Scum like you have no choice in the matter. You're just vermin in my eyes…'

Brooks' face flushed with anger and he rushed at Buchanan, his hands like claws. Before he could attack him, the new prisoner stepped forward and, thrusting his arms out, held Brooks back.

'Don't,' he said. 'It's dangerous to blot your copybook, matey. I've met his type of screw before. He could easily extend your sentence if you physically abuse him. Let him have fun with his words. They're only words, after all. You'll be out on the streets when your time's done – and he'll still be stuck here in his own corrupt world.'

Brooks stared at the stranger for some time as though he was digesting his words. Then suddenly, he pulled back and laughed. 'You're right. While I'm strolling down Piccadilly, popping into a smart tavern for a drink or two, he'll be still here dishing out slops to the inmates in this pigsty.'

The grim sneer on the roseate features of the officer vanished. 'In or out of gaol, you'll still be scum. And you, Harrison, watch it,' he snarled, and he turned abruptly, slamming the door behind him with great force. There followed the grating noise of the key turning in the lock.

In the silence that followed, the two men stared at each other. The newcomer rolled his hand over his shaven head and then held it out for a shake. 'I know your name – that fat ape told me. I'm Harrison, Nigel Harrison.'

Brooks hesitated and then with a stoical twist of the lips, took hold of Harrison's hand.

'Don't worry about me being a nuisance. I'm the quiet as a mouse type. Sorry to invade your territory like, but I gather you're only here for a couple of months.' The voice was light but with an accent that Brooks could not determine.

'Buchanan tell you that, I suppose?'

Harrison nodded. 'Two months, eh? I bet you're counting the days. Me, I've got another eighteen to serve.'

'What for?'

Harrison held up his long fingers and mimed turning an invisible knob. 'Safecracker. One of the best in the business.'

'Really,' said Brooks, smiling.

'Got caught red-handed, as they say, on my last job. I reckon a little runt who held a grudge against me blabbed to the coppers. What a bugger! Just got my hands on a nice lot of sparklers when the coppers rushed in on me.'

'Hard lines.'

'Yeah. So instead of a life of luxury, I get free board and lodgings in this cess pit.'

Brooks shrugged. 'Good at it, are you, the old safe job?'

'The best. Nothing has ever defeated me.'

'What about a Walter and Brennan?'

Harrison chuckled. 'Yeah, they're brutes all right, but I snapped one open in Houndsditch a few years ago. Pity there was small pickings inside. Still, I managed to break open the monster.'

'On the level?'

'I ain't no boaster. What would be the point?'

'What about the Crown Imperial?'

'What, the little green midget things? They're a piece of cake. You could blow on 'em and they'd open.'

Brooks grinned. 'You're right. You obviously know your safes.'

'Well, by the sound of it so do you. Safecracker, too, eh?'

'I am and proud of it.'

Instinctively the two men shook hands again and a strange bond was formed.

'In that case,' said Brooks, flinging himself on his bed, 'welcome to Cell 139. Home sweet bleedin' home.'

'Ta.' Harrison sat on the edge of the spare bed and dropped his small bag of possessions at his feet.

Brooks leaned back, placing his hands behind his head. 'Oh, what I'd give for a fag right now,' he said dreamily. 'Just watching the smoke wander up the ceiling.'

'Well, why didn't you say so?' said Harrison mischievously.

'What you talking about?'

Harrison leaned forward and slipped his long fingers inside the thick woollen sock on his left leg and produced a handful of thin cigarettes. Laying them out on the grey sheet on his bed, he reached down into his right sock and produced a slim box of lucifers.

'What the hell!' cried Brooks, his eyes wide with amazement. 'How did you get those?'

Harrison smiled. 'I have my methods. Got my chap Johnny on the outside keeps me supplied with my wants. He comes and brings me magic food parcels. Cakes that contain booze, pies with hidden secrets like cigarettes. That sort of thing. Here, enjoy a smoke.' He passed a cigarette and a match to Brooks who took them eagerly and lit up. Harrison followed suit and they remained silent for some time, filling the small cell with a fine pungent fug of tobacco smoke.

'You're quite a resourceful fellow, ain't you?' observed Brooks at length.

Harrison's eyes twinkled brightly. 'I like to think so. In fact I reckon I'm so resourceful that I don't intend to stay caged up in this place for too long. It's my intention to get out of here round about the time you'll be flying the coop.'

'Escape, you mean?'

'Yes.'

'You'll never get away with it.'

'Oh, yes I will. The security here is as sloppy as Irish stew. With some outside help from my comrade Johnny, it will be a piece of cake.'

'How you gonna do it?'

Harrison touched the side of his nose with a long forefinger. 'Now that would be telling. I'm not stupid enough to share that little secret with anyone. Secrets have a habit of revealing themselves.'

Brooks gave an indignant shrug of the shoulders. 'Please yourself, but I hope you're not suggesting I'd blab your plans to the screws.'

''Course not. It's not that I don't trust you – a seasoned felon like yourself, but I do think it best if I play my cards as close as I can to my chest.'

'Fair enough. I wish you luck. If you make it, we should meet up and I'll buy you a drink.'

'That, my friend, is a date.'

Two days later Brooks and Harrison, who had bonded in friendship in the interim, were in the prison canteen at lunchtime queuing up for the brown mush that professed to be shepherd's pie, when Buchanan waddled down the line and stopped by Brooks.

'I heard that,' he snapped, grabbing Brooks by the collar and yanking him from the line.

'Heard what? I said nothing,' protested Brooks forcefully.

'Oh, yes you did. You were being disrespectful to an officer – namely me.'

'Disrespectful? Again, I said nothing.'

'Don't you lie to me. You called me "scum" again. I heard you.'

Brooks shook his head vigorously, his face reddening with suppressed anger.

'He is telling the truth,' said Harrison but Buchanan ignored him.

'So, Brooksey, insubordination again. For that you've just lost your privilege for lunch. No grub for you. I'll just take you back to your cell.' Buchanan reached out to grab hold of the prisoner's arm, but Brooks swiped it away and let out a feral roar, his eyes bulging with fury. With speed, he landed a punch hard in Buchanan's midriff. Giving a deep groan, the officer's bulky body folded in two and he staggered backwards. Brooks moved forward and hit him again, this time hard in the face. Blood squirted from his nose, minute scarlet droplets spraying into the air. Buchanan groaned once more and sank to his knees but before Brooks could go in for the kill, he was restrained by two other officers who had raced to the scene.

Buchanan clambered unsteadily to his feet and strangely he was grinning broadly. 'You've gone and done it now, ain't you? An unprovoked attack on a prison officer. Blotted that pristine copybook book of yours. You can say goodbye to your imminent release now, Brooksey. I reckon you've added another six months to your sentence, my lad.' He laughed heartily as blood trickled down his chin and on to his jacket. 'Alright, boys take him to solitary. Forty-eight hours in there should help to cool the bastard down.'

Initially Brooks was lost for words as the two officers dragged him off, but Harrison could see the despair in his eyes as he realised what his hot temper had provoked him to do and the consequences of his actions. As he reached the door of the canteen, the eyes of all the other prisoners on him, he let out a long, fearful plaintive cry: 'No.' The sound of it faded away as he was taken from the room.

Chapter Twenty-two

Harrison had just returned from his duties in the food store and was lying on his bed staring meditatively at the ceiling when the door of the cell opened and the cowed figure of Jacob Brooks stumbled in. He was drawn and his gaunt features were even paler than usual.

'You got any snout left?' he said, ghosting his way to his bed and sitting hunched up on the edge.

'Sure,' said Harrison, leaning forward and feeling under the foot of his mattress. He retrieved a couple of cigarettes and a match. 'I'll join you,' he said.

'Ta, mate.'

'Was it bad in there?' asked Harrison, lighting up.

'Not really. Tedious and boring. No light, no food. That isn't what gave me pain. It was the thought of another six months in here. Me and my bloody temper. But it was that dog Buchanan who goaded me.'

'Of course it was,' observed Harrison. 'He was getting you back for the other day. He knew if he pushed you enough, you'd fly off the handle and attack like you nearly did in here, until I stopped you.'

'Yeah, you're right. Pity you didn't try and stop me in the canteen.'

'I'd no chance there. I didn't want to end up solitary myself for by getting involved. Old Buchanan was on a mission to get you. Anything I did wouldn't have stopped him.'

'Yeah, you're right. It was best you kept out of it I suppose. Anyway, it's official. I saw the Guv'nor just now, they've topped up my sentence up by six months because I've been a naughty boy. Bleedin' hell! What can I do?'

'Escape with me.'

Brooks laughed. 'You must be joking. And get caught and find myself with even more time to spend in here.'

'Just a thought,' said Harrison, rubbing his scalp. 'It's up to you of course, but I'm due to make the break next Tuesday.'

'Good luck to you, mate. I'll see you at breakfast on Wednesday.' Brooks gave a hollow laugh and leaned back on his bed and blew some smoke up to the ceiling of the cell.

Harrison hooded his eyes and smiled to himself.

The prison was never quiet, even in the watches of the night. There was banging, singing, cries of anger or sorrow and even weird wailing sounds as though a kind of strange ritual was being performed somewhere. The noises echoed along the grim narrow corridors so that there were always the persistent unsettling background reverberations in the air. It was a mode of life that prisoners had to get used to, if not actually come to terms with.

In Cell 139 that night, the raucous sounds were helping to keep Jacob Brooks awake; that and his anguish at having his sentence extended. It was only by six months, he reasoned, but it really was beyond his limit of endurance. He had promised the Organisation that he would be free for action within two months. They had welcomed the news, inviting him back into the fold, the one controlled by the new Master. He really couldn't afford to keep them waiting. They wouldn't tolerate such an inconvenience. He would be dropped from their schemes. He would be out on his own again, having to fend for himself rather than being part of a well-oiled criminal machine which looked after its own.

There was no doubt about it: he had to get out. He knew there was only one way to achieve this. He had to escape.

'You awake, Harrison?' he said, his voice just above a whisper.

'Just about,' came the muted response in darkness.

'I need a favour. A bloody big favour.'

'Sorry chum, I'm right out of smokes now.'

'No, it's not a cigarette I'm after. It's something more important.'

'Like what?'

'I want to make a break for it with you, like you said.' Brooks blurted it out in an instant.

Harrison did not reply.

'Did you hear me?'

'Yeah,' Harrison said at length. 'You want to join me when I make my escape.'

'That's it. Will you help me?'

'I don't know. You said no when I suggested it. Giving it some thought, I'm not so sure…'

'Come on, mate. If one can do it, surely two can.'

'Easy said. It's double the risk. And you've shown yourself to be a bit unpredictable, fly off the handle. I need a cool head in a venture like this.'

Another protracted silence.

'What do you say, eh? I'm desperate and when I'm on a job I'm focused.'

'What's in it for me? I'll be risking a lot.'

Brooks pulled himself up and sat on the edge of the bed, ruffling his fingers through his matted hair. 'Look... look...' he rasped, and then stopped desperately trying to come up with an answer that would win Harrison over to his idea.

'We're mates, aren't we? I'll see you right,' he said at length.

'We're mates while we share this cell but it could be another thing on the outside – if we get outside.'

'You seemed so confident about your escape plan... I'll fall in with all you tell me to do. Once we're free... I'll ... I'll get you a situation with my lot. I'll get you into the Organisation. They'll look after you. You'll never need to scrabble for jobs on your own again, how's that?'

'How can you be sure?'

'I can. Trust me.'

'Trust... a fragile thing in this world.'

'I may be a crook, a thief, but I am a man of my word. Please help me, Harrison.'

Harrison yawned. 'Very well. We'll do it together – but I'll hold you to your promise.'

'You won't regret it, I can tell you. Believe me, you've made a smart move.'

'Maybe I have,' said Harrison lightly. In the darkness, Brooks could not see the satisfied smile on his companion's face.

* * *

It was mid-morning and Harrison was working in the food store, checking the cans of meat when an officer informed him he was wanted in the governor's office.

'What for?'

'Never you mind,' growled the officer. 'Follow me.'

Minutes later he was admitted to the governor's office. The head of the prison, a prim sandy-haired man in his fifties with a shiny face and neat features was sitting at his desk. Behind him, standing with his back to the room staring out of the window was a neatly dressed, well-built man. As door closed behind Harrison, the man turned round and smiled. So did Harrison. 'Johnny, my dear fellow,' he cried, steeping forward and grabbing the man by the hand.

Chapter Twenty-three

In Baker Street that night, three men sat around the dining table after sampling a light supper. The candles were burning low and it was only towards the end of the meal that the conversation turned to what they were there for – for what had been on their mind for days.

'So, Watson,' said Mycroft Holmes, leaning back in his chair and lighting a large cigar, 'brother Sherlock believes that I did choose the right man for the job?

'Without a doubt,' replied Watson. 'He is very pleased with the ways things are going at the moment. Brooks has proved to be reliably volatile.'

'I'm not surprised,' said Mycroft, 'I spent some hours studying the file containing the members of Moriarty's gang before I selected that fellow. And then of course I had to pull a few strings with the prison service in order for this extremely dangerous scheme to be instigated.'

'Well, according to Holmes, all seems to be going smoothly,' said Watson encouragingly.

'Going smoothly *so far*, my dear doctor... or should I call you Johnny? However, let me remind you of the old adage that there is many a slip 'twixt cup and lip. There is still the matter of the escape.'

'Ah, yes,' said Lestrade somewhat gloomily, lighting a cigarette. 'That is a hell of a hurdle. If it goes wrong the whole plan is wrecked.'

At this observation, the three men fell silent.

Chapter Twenty-four

ℰ

'I hear you've been up to the Guv'nor's office today,' said Brooks. It was a casual statement but Harrison sensed the underlying suspicion it carried.

Harrison gave a little laugh. 'Yes. I'm afraid I've been caught out.'

'What d'you mean?'

'My food parcel. I get one every month from my mother.'

'Your mother?'

'Well, not really. It's supposed to be from my mother but it comes from my old mate, Johnny. Hence the cigarettes you and I have been enjoying. You know, I told you: he secretes little treats in a group of innocent items. Usually I get away with it, but not this time. You know how the screws examine any packages. Nosey blighters. Usually Johnny is too clever for them, but not this time. They found a small bottle of rum in a fruit cake and a short bladed knife in a prayer book.'

'A prayer book!'

'Oh, yes, when it comes to smuggling in merchandise, I'm a religious chap, didn't you know?'

Brooks giggled. 'Well, bless you, my son.'

Both men laughed.

'So they got all your stuff, eh?'

'Not all. They let me have this.' Harrison reached under his bed and pulled out a large book.

'What's that then?'

'It is a tome that lives up to its title.'

'Which is?'

'*Great Expectations* by Mr Charles Dickens.'

'*Great Expectations*?'

'It all relates to our escape. I have great expectations that it will be successful.'

'How does the book help?'

'What the eagled eyes officers failed to spot when they examined my mother's package of goodies was what is slipped down the inside of the spine: a quantity of notes of the realm to be used for the purpose of bribes – four twenty-pound notes.'

'I think it's about time you told me the whole story regarding this escape plan. If we're going soon, I need to be clued up.'

'You're quite right, especially as we leave on Tuesday.'

'Only five days away.'

'Yes. This time next week we'll be free men.'

'So, give me the lowdown.'

'Right, listen carefully. The supply van comes on Tuesday with provisions for the week. I have got friendly with the driver, a cove named Archie Leach. He's done time himself in the past so he knows the score. With the promise of a crisp twenty-pound note, I've persuaded him to let me slip inside the back of his van after all the stuff has been unloaded and he's ready to leave. He's such a regular at the prison that he says they never inspect the van as it goes out through the gate. If we did get caught, or he's suspected of helping with an escape, he can easily plead ignorance, knowing nothing about his illegal passengers.'

'What about the screw on duty down in the stores?'

'Bony Johnson. Yes, well that's one little problem I'll have to leave you to deal with. You'll have to make your way down to the prison stores on your own. Pretend you have a message for Bony. Just administer a gentle bump on the head. Nothing drastic. Give him a headache, that's all. We don't want a dead man on our hands. He's a gentle soul really, you'll have no problem dealing with him.'

Brooks nodded. 'I know the bloke. I can handle him, no problem. Won't this Leach chap wonder where Bony is?'

Harrison shook his head. 'No, he usually finds himself at a quiet area down behind the shelves with a paper and a cigarette. Let me do all the work. He won't be missed. Once the goods are unloaded, I'll pretend to get the papers signed by Bony and then we simply slip into the back of the wagon and pray.'

'Sounds like a piece of cake.'

'Don't get too confident, my friend, cake sometimes has a habit of crumbling.'

Tuesday morning: the day of the escape.

Harrison reported early to the food store and to his surprise and dismay he found Officer Buchanan in situ.

'Early bird, ain't you, Harrison?' he sneered as he puffed on a cigarette. 'Hoping to slip some goodies into your back pocket?'

'Good morning, Officer Buchanan,' Harrison replied civilly. 'Where is Officer Johnson?'

'Bony? He's not too well this morning. In sick bay. Something nasty to do with his stomach – so you have the pleasure of my company today.'

Harrison gave a gentle nod of the head, while he was thinking hard. The presence of Buchanan was certainly a rather nasty unexpected fly in the ointment. He would be not as easy to fool or deal with as Johnson, who was a pleasant enough fellow, possessing none of the violent belligerence of Buchanan. To some extent Bony felt sorry for the inmates, whereas Buchanan exhibited a ferocious hated of his charges.

But here he was, standing before him, his posture aggressive and arrogant. Harrison realised that there was no way he could alert Brooks to this new and threatening situation. When he appeared unexpectedly in the stores, no doubt Buchanan's suspicions would be aroused immediately.

Buchanan pulled up a chair and planted his bulky body on it. 'Well, don't let me stop you getting on with your duties, Harrison. I'm only here to keep an eye on things, not to dirty my hands.' He gave a raw self-satisfied chuckle.

'Well, I have to clear some shelves in readiness for the new delivery. That's at ten thirty.'

'Off you go then.'

Harrison disappeared down one of the four narrow aisles of shelves stocked with provisions on three levels. The situation was a tricky one. It was clear to him that Buchanan had to be dealt with before both Brooks and the delivery van arrived. If Buchanan smelt a rat and raised the alarm, the whole scheme would fall apart. He hadn't much time in which to act.

* * *

Moments later, just as Buchanan was about to light another cigarette, he heard a cry from somewhere amongst the rows of provisions. 'Officer Buchanan, come here quickly, there is something strange…'

The officer gave an irritated growl, pinched the end of the cigarette and slipped it back in his top pocket. What was this Harrison oaf on about now? he pondered as he rose from the chair and made his way down one of the gloomy aisles of food stuffs. 'Where are you?' he bellowed.

There was no reply.

'Harrison, where the hell are you?' he called again as he wandered further down the aisle. 'If you're playing games with me, you'll be sorry…'

Suddenly he felt a violent blow on the back of his head, which sent his hat spinning into the air. He staggered forward, vision blurring as jagged bright lights danced before his eyes. Reaching out in desperation, Buchanan's hand grasped one of the lower shelves. With luck he managed to steady himself, halting his descent to the ground.

Harrison was dismayed to see the brute regain his upright position. With a grunt Buchanan turned to face him. His features were suffused with rage.

'Why, you bastard,' he roared, spittle flying from his lips, as he lunged forward.

Harrison raised the stout section of shelving which he had used to deliver the blow. Before he was able to use it again, Buchanan had wrenched it from his grasp. In a swift, savage motion, he brought it down towards Harrison's shoulders. With a lithe dance step, Harrison feinted sideways, avoiding the blow. Deftly swinging his leg high, he managed to bring his boot into hard contact with the officer's stomach. Buchanan gave a sharp groan of pain but it did not stop his advance. He struck out again with the piece of wood. Harrison dropped to the ground and then quickly slithered through the officer's legs. In an instant he was able to spring up behind the man.

For a moment Buchanan was baffled as to where his opponent had gone. Harrison tapped him gently on the shoulder. As the brute turned round, he landed a hard right-handed upper cut to his jaw. This time Buchanan sank to his knees. Harrison wasted no time in swinging his leg with great force again. This time his toe cap connected directly with his opponent's chin. There was a crunch of bone and blood dribbled from his mouth. With a groan, he fell back and lay still in an awkward heap on the floor. His eyelids fluttered erratically and then suddenly flipped open. The staring eyes were wild with fury. Harrison realised that the beast was still not down and out. As he lifted up his leg to deliver what he hoped would be the final blow, Buchanan grabbed it in his large hands and twisted hard. Harrison gave a yelp of pain, lost his balance and hit the hard stone floor. Within seconds, his opponent had scrambled to his feet and was standing over him menacingly, the blood still spilling from his mouth.

Harrison pulled back and sprang to his feet. He gritted his teeth as he desperately tried to remember what his old Baritsu teacher had taught him. In his mind's eye he visualised the dusty room where he trained, the sunlight spilling through the slatted window blinds. Chu Sen had patiently demonstrated the cunning moves which could, with perfected ease and skill, defeat any opponent. It was with these deft and fluid manipulations that one could overcome an assailant, however bulky their stature. He had used them with Moriarty on the ledge overlooking the Falls and successfully defeated him. However, the Professor was older, and less muscled and resilient than the great ox who was bearing down on him with malevolence in his eyes.

Now was the time. Harrison flexed himself. He sidestepped the advancing Buchanan, while at the same time grasping his right arm in a firm hold. Bending his own frame slightly, putting extra pressure on the balls of his feet, he exerted all his effort to lift his opponent into the air. He held him aloft briefly before thrusting him down on the ground with great force. Buchanan landed hard on his back, his head making violent contact with the stone floor. With a chesty exhalation, his body froze and he sank into unconsciousness.

Harrison stared down at him, waiting to see if the officer exhibited any movement. There was none. He really was defeated this time.

'That was very nifty. You certainly know how to handle yourself.'

Harrison looked up and saw Jacob Brooks leaning against the shelves at the end of the aisle. He wore a smug smile on his face.

'And how long have you been there?'

'Long enough to see you put our fat friend to sleep.'

'And it didn't cross your mind to help me?'

Brooks gave a slight shrug. 'You seemed to be doing perfectly all right on your own.'

Harrison clenched his fist. He wanted to knock this cocky devil down but he had enough sense and self-control to know that such an action would be counter-productive to his plans.

'Well,' he said, 'you can at least help me tie Buchanan up and gag him.'

'Happy to oblige.'

'Then we need to stow him out of sight before Archie arrives with the van.'

The two men set about this task with alacrity. Harrison secured a length of rope from one of the packing crates. Rubbing the rope along the sharp end of the wooden case, he was able to split it in two. With one piece he bound the officer's hands behind his back and the other was used to secure his legs. Brooks had found a large old duster which he wrapped around the unconscious man's mouth.

'That should keep the old devil silent,' he grinned, pulling the knot tight.

'Let's hope he stays unconscious until we're well away. Right now, let's stow him at the far end of the furthest aisle.'

They dragged the hefty man to his resting place under a rack of shelves, and covered it with an old piece of tarpaulin.

Brooks made the sign of the cross and giggled. 'May the old bastard rest in peace.'

Walking back to the main area of the food store, Harrison consulted the old clock on the wall. It was ten o'clock. Fifteen minutes before the delivery van was due. He heaved a sigh before announcing quietly, 'All we have to do now is wait...'

Chapter Twenty-five

❧

At a quarter past ten on the dot, there came the noise of the unlocking of the large double doors to the food store. The clanking sound echoed through the large chamber. Harrison gave Brooks a gentle shove on the shoulder. 'Hide yourself now.' Brooks made his way down the furthest aisle, dropped to the floor and slipped himself under one of the shelves at the far end.

The ancient hinges groaned as the portal gradually swung open. A caped police offer, Sergeant Amos Pringle by name, stepped through first, a pistol in hand. It was held casually – there was no intention to use it. He was a veteran of this procedure and familiarity had bred if not contempt, then an expectation that there was nothing to be concerned about. This was just routine. On seeing Harrison, he waved in greeting, and then gestured for Archie Leach to bring the loaded horse-drawn wagon through the gate into the food store.

Archie gently encouraged the old grey horse to clip-clop its way into the chamber. Once safely inside, Pringle approached Harrison. 'Still on duty here, I see,' he said, in a friendly fashion.

'Yes, sir.'

'Where's Bony?'

'He's off sick. Stomach trouble. Officer Buchanan is in charge today.'

Pringle looked around. 'Can't see him.'

'He's just popped out to the lavatory.'

Pringle was not the sort of man to openly criticise a fellow officer, although he had a very low opinion of Buchanan, but he allowed himself a deprecating roll of the eyes. 'Well, I am sure he can trust you, Harrison. At least you know what you're doing. I'll leave you to get on with things. Archie will bang on the door as usual when you've finished.'

After Pringle had left, locking the doors, Archie Leach came down from the driving seat and approached Harrison. He was a wiry sixty-year-old with a wild thatch of grey hair and a heavily lined face which spoke of a lifetime of hardship. 'Is it still on for today?' he said in a hoarse whisper, while his eyes swept the building.

Harrison nodded.

'You sure? You know the risks – and remember, I am the innocent ignorant party in all this if things go awry.'

'Of course. But I'll have a companion with me.'

Pringle's features clouded. 'That wasn't part of the deal.'

'It will make no difference to our plans. It doesn't mean we have to do anything different, but to ease your worry, I'm happy to double your fee.'

'Double it?' The man thought for a moment. 'Very well then, but before we go any further, you'd better let me have your passport.' He rubbed his thumb and forefinger of his right hand together in an avaricious gesture.

Harrison reached into the back pocket of his trousers and produced two twenty-pound notes. Pringle slipped them neatly into his smock, his blue eyes twinkling with pleasure. 'Where is this other cove then?'

'He's hiding at the moment. I'll bring him out when we're ready to go.'

'Have it as you like, but first things first,' Pringle announced in a business-like manner. 'We need to get the stuff off the van.' He returned to the vehicle, unleashing the canvas drape at the rear to reveal the goods ready to be unloaded.

This laborious procedure took about thirty minutes. Pringle passed the various canisters and sacks from the back of the van to Harrison, who bore them away to their various places down the aisles. Both men worked in silence, the tension growing as the risks they were about to take grew closer. Harrison hoped that Buchanan would remain immobile until they had completed the task.

When all the produce was stowed away, Pringle guided the horse so that the van turned round and was ready to pass through the exit once the doors were opened. Then Harrison summoned Brooks from his hiding place and, without a word, he clambered into the back of the van and covered himself with some sacking.

'I will have to remain visible to Pringle when he opens the doors or he will grow suspicious,' Harrison informed Leach. 'I'll give him a wave and pretend to attend to some duty down one of the aisles. You engage him in some pleasantry while I double back out of sight and get into the van.'

Leach nodded, clambered down from the driver's seat and hammered on the doors. Some moments later, they swung open and Officer Pringle stepped into view.

'Job done, eh?' he cried.

'All is safely gathered in,' grinned Harrison, with a wave before disappearing down one of the aisles. Here he waited a few seconds before crouching low and making his way back to the rear of the van. As he did so he could hear the muted conversation between Leach and Pringle. Pushing aside the flap he pulled himself up and slipped inside. Moments later, the van began to move forward.

'We did it,' whispered Brooks in the darkness.

'Shut up. We're not out of the woods yet.'

They heard the large wooden door close and the turn of the key. Now there were just the prison gates themselves and then they would be beyond the confines of the prison.

The van rocked gently as it progressed. And then they heard a voice call out: 'Stop. I say, stop!' It was Officer Pringle's voice.

Both men froze.

'What the hell,' croaked Brooks, but Harrison clasped a hand over his mouth.

The van shuddered to a halt. 'Is something the matter?' asked Leach, tentatively. Harrison could hear a slight tremble in his voice.

'Being a bit careless today, Mr Leach, aren't we?' said Pringle.

'Are we...?'

'You haven't secured your flap at the rear of the van.'

'Ain't I?' The voice sounded nervous to those with an ear to hear it.

'Not like you.'

'No, no, it ain't.'

There was a long pause and then Pringle spoke again: 'Well, aren't you going to attend to it?'

'Oh, yes, of course, of course.' Leach's voice was now almost a whisper. Harrison heard him step down from the driving seat and move to the rear of the van.

'Do you need a hand?' asked Pringle.

'No, no. I can manage.'

In the darkness Harrison and Brooks lay still as they saw the canvas flap tighten while Leach secured the straps.

There was a long period of quiet and then the van began moving again. Pringle muttered something, but Leach did not respond.

Moments later there was the casual formality of checking the driver's papers by the officer at the prison gates before the van was allowed to pass through beyond the walls of the prison.

'We've done it,' exclaimed Brooks in hushed tones. 'We're free.'

Chapter Twenty-six

Doctor Watson tore open the telegram and read the contents with mixed emotions. He was pleased yet apprehensive at the news it carried. The telegram read simply:

THEY HAVE ESCAPED STOP MH

Chapter Twenty-seven

As evening began to fall on the city of London, Harrison and Brooks were making their way on foot to the area of Southwark, south of the river. They had left the van some three miles from the prison, much to the relief of Archie Leach, who was more than happy to see the back of them. He had pulled to the side of a quiet lane and unfastened the canvas flap at the rear of the van.

'Alright, skedaddle,' he growled, his voice tense and humourless. It was clear to Harrison as he studied the man's strained features that he was regretting getting involved in the project, realising now that pleas of ignorance may not wash with the police when the prisoners' disappearance was discovered. Harrison felt sorry for the fellow, but Brooks appeared oblivious of the older man's angst.

They were now making their way to what Brooks called the Dormitory: a resting place for members of the Organisation who needed a refuge for a time. It was here, Brooks informed Harrison, that he would be able to contact with one of the main men, a certain Colonel Moran. It would be he that would arrange for Harrison to be formally enrolled in the gang.

As they walked, Brooks began reminiscing about 'the old days' when 'that wily cove, the Professor' was in charge.

'Did you ever meet him?' asked Harrison.

'Just the once. Odd kind of bird. He was like an old-fashioned school master – tall, with hunched shoulders and a wheezy way of speaking. However, the strangest thing about him was the way he kept moving his head from side to side like he was watching every corner of the room for something. But he was a clever fellow – a genius, I reckon. I thought we'd never see his like again.'

'And have you? Seen his like again?' asked Harrison, keeping the eagerness from his voice.

'Yes, I reckon so. She has organised the troops with remarkable efficiency…'

'She!'

Brooks widened his eyes with apprehension. He realised that perhaps he'd said more than he should. He lapsed into silence.

Harrison prompted him. 'You said "she". Are you saying that the new head of the Organisation is a woman?'

Brooks did not reply.

'Come on. After all we've been through you owe me the truth. You can tell me.'

'I should have kept my big mouth shut.'

'Why? If I'm to join the Organisation, I'm bound to find out sooner or later.'

'Not necessarily. It's supposed to be a secret. You're not a member yet. And not all the members know. She likes to remain in the shadows.'

I'll wager she does, thought Harrison. 'Well, now you've let the cat out of the bag, tell me more.'

'There's nothing more to tell.'

'Of course there is. Who is she?'

'I don't know exactly.'

'What *do* you know? How on earth did this mysterious female get to be in charge of the Organisation?'

'I'm not sure. I heard she had some connection with Moriarty.'

Harrison repressed a smile. 'Some connection? What connection?'

Brooks gave a huge shrug. 'I've no idea. Look, I've said more than I should. The less you know the safer it is for you. Men have woken up to find their throats cut for asking too many questions. Now forget it.'

Forget it? There was no chance of that, thought Harrison.

They carried on walking, moving along the riverbank beyond Blackfriars Bridge, until they came to a tall, weathered warehouse building which looked from the outside as though it was derelict. The name Beaumont's Warehouse in very faded lettering was just visible on the wall. Brooks led his companion to a small door at the side of the building. Here he knocked hard. It had a strange staccato rhythm which Harrison realised was a code. In time, one of the small panels in the door opened and a grizzly face materialised there and peered out.

'The night is dark without the stars,' intoned Brooks.

Immediately the panel was replaced and the sound of the lock turning was followed by the opening of the door. There stood the squat bearded gatekeeper with a pistol in his hand.

'Name and business.' The voice was deep and rich in Irish brogue.

'I'm Jacob Brooks. You'll have my name on the list. I've been involved in the Organisation for some years. We need shelter for a few days, just broken out of the nick with my associate here and then I need to see the Colonel.'

'Oh, yes, I know you, Brooksey. Very nimble, your mitts are, where safes are concerned.'

He grinned. 'Yeah, that's me.'

'And the other bloke?' growled the bearded one.

'A new recruit. A legitimate fellow with skills useful to the Organisation. Trust me.'

The gatekeeper stared at them for a few moments and then beckoned them inside with the barrel of his revolver.

'I'm Mullaney, but everyone calls me Irish. Welcome, lads. We've only got one other inmate here at the moment and he's abed nursing his wounds after falling foul in a bar fight.'

'All we need are beds and grub and ale if you've got some,' said Brooks.

Irish nodded. 'I'll take you up to the kitchen and Mrs Doherty will sort you out.'

'And...' Brooks leaned forward and touched Irish's arm, 'if you'll get a message to the Colonel. I'd really like to see him.'

'I will, I will,' murmured Irish.

Brooks and Harrison were led up a dark rickety staircase to a room on the first floor which served as a kitchen area. Here a plump middle-aged lady was sitting on one chair with her feet up on another, smoking a clay pipe. She looked up casually as the three men entered.

'Got some hungry and thirsty customers for you, Daisy.'

'All my customers are hungry and thirsty,' replied Daisy Doherty as she rose to her feet. 'Evenin' gents. How does sausages and mash along with a pint of ale sound?'

'It sounds good,' grinned Brooks. 'Bound to be better than the prison slop we've been used to, eh, Harrison?'

'Definitely,' his companion agreed.

'Right, lads, sit yourself down at the table and I'll bring you the drinks. The food will be along a little later.'

The two men did as they were bidden.

'Right, I'll leave you to it,' said Irish, heading for the door. 'The sleeping quarters is one floor up. Help yourself to any empty bed.'

'Don't forget about the Colonel,' advised Brooks.

'Don't you fret. I'll make sure he knows you want to see him. Enjoy your grub.' With these parting words he disappeared.

After consuming the meal and the ale both men decided to retire. 'It's been a long day,' observed Brooks with a yawn.

Harrison lay awake that night, thinking over what he had learned regarding this mysterious female who apparently was now controlling the actions of the Organisation. Brooks' careless disclosure had been an exciting revelation, confirming his suspicions. Harrison reasoned that if the woman had a close connection with Moriarty, an emotional attachment to him in some way, it would explain why he had been targeted and taunted by her and her cronies. It could be that she was seeking revenge for the death of the Professor. In all his research into the Professor's criminal life, he had discovered virtually nothing of his personal biography. The wily bird had covered his tracks well, apart from the French connection, the payments to the conservatoire.

He did not know if Moriarty had any living family. It was unlikely that this woman, whom Harrison had begun to think of as Madame X, would be Moriarty's wife or sister. He felt sure he would have been aware of her in his investigations into the Professor's activities when he was compiling a dossier on the Organisation for Scotland Yard three years previously. There was not a scrap of evidence that there was a wife or family lurking in the background. Such a domestic scenario seemed highly improbable. Moriarty was the sort of man who would regard a wife as an encumbrance, a hindrance to his criminal ambitions. As for sisters, this was a closed book to him. It certainly was a possibility that his old enemy had a sister but if this was the case, why had she waited such a long time to act?

There were still many questions to be answered regarding Madame X. He needed more data before he could solve this intriguing riddle. That would come in time. He had known when he started this plan that it would be a long game. He had to be patient.

With this thought stowed away, he drifted off into deep sleep.

Chapter Twenty-eight

While Harrison fell asleep and Big Ben boomed the hour of midnight over the great city, in Moriarty's headquarters, the new mistress of the Organisation was staring at the late edition of the *Evening Standard*.

'I want it. I must have it,' she purred. 'It will be the first great coup of the revived Moriarty Organisation. The phoenix will rise in glory. It will establish me as queen of the criminal world and with that will come more power.' She stabbed her finger at a photograph on the front page. Colonel Sebastian Moran leaned over to gain a view of the grainy image. It appeared to be a large precious stone set as the main feature of an elaborate necklace.

'A pretty thing,' he observed.

'Pretty, priceless, and symbolic. It is Josephine's necklace as presented to her by Napoleon Bonaparte. It is a diplomatic loan, due to be shipped to England in a fortnight's time and worn by Queen Victoria at a grand dinner. It is a gesture by the French in an attempt to improve our uneasy relations with France. Its theft while on English soil will certainly throw the cat amongst the pigeons. The discomfiture between the two nations will provide a pleasing catalyst. Who knows what chain of circumstances may follow, and what advantages may present themselves for the Organisation?'

'I see,' said Moran stroking his chin. 'Certainly, things have been a little sticky with the Frenchies over the Nile business. I know they want us out of Egypt but we're hanging on in there, much to their chagrin.' He allowed himself a brief chuckle. 'This necklace business must be some kind of sop, hoping to soften us. I doubt it will wash with Her Majesty.'

'Indeed, but for the moment the key point of interest to us is to procure the necklace. Any further benefits will result from that. The British ambassador Edmund Monson will accompany the trinket to England where it will be stored in a vault at the City and Counties Bank until the day of the grand dinner. I intend to steal it.'

Moran's eyes widened. 'Do you, by Jove! And how are you going to manage that?'

'With ease, I would suggest. Our informant at the Palace has informed me that in reality the necklace is to be stored secretly, not in the headquarters of the bank in the Strand as announced, but lodged elsewhere. A temporary home until the dinner. I'll extract further details from Sir Gregory regarding the exact location and the security arrangements, but I will treat the affair as a standard robbery. No one will be expecting an attempt to steal the necklace from this insignificant secret locale, especially when they have gone to all the trouble of creating the impression that it is nestling in the bank's headquarters. The theft will come as a great surprise to all. It will clearly inform the authorities that the Moriarty

Organisation is back in business – big business.'

Moran cast an admiring glance at this remarkable woman.

It was two days later when Jacob Brooks received a message from Colonel Moran. 'I am to meet him alone by the lake in St James's Park at three this afternoon,' he informed Harrison. 'And before you ask, I am to go alone.'

Harrison gave an understanding nod. 'But you will tell him about me. Get me a berth aboard ship.'

'Of course. I don't think they'll be any problem when I tell him how resourceful you are and what skills you have with your pinkies.' He held up his own hand and wiggled his fingers.

Harrison smiled. One step nearer, he mused.

As it was a warm afternoon, St James's Park was busy with Londoners taking advantage of the sunshine. Colonel Sebastian Moran was seated on a bench at the lake side opposite West Island. He was smoking a cigar in a lazy fashion. Since he had shaved off his grizzled moustache, and had begun wearing spectacles with tinted lenses, he felt invulnerable. No policeman who had seen the his grainy identification photograph when he had been arrested after the Empty House affair would recognise him now. No one, apart from those members of the Organisation whom he might consider intimates. Jacob Brooks did not quite fall into that category, but Moran had had many dealings with the expert safecracker in the past and was more than happy to bring him back into the fold, especially if the lady's audacious scheme was to come to fruition. If a safe was to be opened, Brooks was the man and Moran needed to be certain of him after some months out of the Organisation.

As he stared out at the calm waters of the lake, the warmth of the sun on his face, he felt at ease with himself and the world. Gradually he closed his eyes and then he sensed a shadow falling over him. He looked up and saw the figure of Jacob Brooks standing there. He had spruced himself up since he had last encountered him. He now wore a natty second-hand tweed suit, a clean collarless shirt with a woollen flat cap perched on his head, the neb worn low over the forehead, shadowing his features.

'Colonel Moran, Brooks reporting for duty, sir,' he said jovially, giving a mock salute.

Moran was not amused.

'Sit down, man,' he snapped, 'and do not use my name in public.'

Brooks shrank a little and obeyed the order.

'So, as I said in my message, I made it out of gaol and am ready for action. I hope you'll receive me back into the Organisation.'

Moran gave a curt nod. 'There will always be a place for people like you with your peculiar talents.' He paused. 'Provided you keep your mouth shut. Where are you now?'

Brooks cleared his throat. There was no mistaking the look the Colonel gave him. 'Kipping down at the Dormitory.'

'Find your own quarters and let Irish know where you are. He keeps a record of all our "employees". I've no doubt we'll be calling on your services before long.'

'There's my associate as well…'

'Associate?'

'The fellow who organised the escape. A good bloke. Clever. Sharp mind. He's a safecracker, too. He wants to join the team.'

'Does he?'

'Yeah, a fellow named Harrison. Nigel Harrison.'

'Trustworthy?'

'Sure. He got me out of the prison.'

'I'll need to see him. Is he also at the Dormitory?'

Brooks nodded.

'I'll call there in three days' time at seven. Tell Irish to find a room for us. In the meantime I'll need to check the man out.'

'Sure. But you won't be disappointed.'

'We'll see.' Moran dropped the butt of his cigar on the ground and rose from the bench. Without another word he strolled away in the direction of the Mall.

Promptly at seven p.m. three days later, Irish showed Harrison into a small room on the ground floor of the Dormitory. The chamber, with one small window facing a brick wall, was dimly lit by a few candles, and housed just a desk and two chairs. Sitting behind the desk in the flickering amber gloom was a man Harrison knew well. He prayed that his alibi, carefully constructed by Mycroft, had stood up to investigation, and that the man did not recognise him. His extreme disguise was effective; the shaved head, the discoloured false teeth, the bristling moustache, the goatee beard and the self-imposed scar on the cheek would fool most people, but Moran was not most people. They had been at close quarters and as a successful hunter the Colonel had a keen eye. This was the greatest challenge of his dissembling life. If he failed here not only would his plan crumble but his life would not be worth a pin's fee.

A drift of cigar smoke sailed across Moran's features as he gestured to Harrison to take the seat opposite him.

'Do sit yourself down, my good fellow,' he purred. 'I just want a little chat.'

'Thank you, sir.'

'My comrade Brooks says you wish to join us.'

'Indeed, sir.'

'He says that you have certain skills which may be of use to us, and my enquiries about you suggest that this is so.'

'I am a fine hand at cracking a safe, if I say so myself.'

'Better than your friend Brooks?'

'Well, it's not my place to say, but I reckon I could match him any day.'

Moran leaned forward and produced a small wooden box from a shelf beneath the desk.

'Are you up for a test, Mr Harrison?'

'Surely,' came the casual reply.

Moran opened the box and extracted a square of metal, at the centre of which was a combination dial from a safe.

'This is a clever device constructed by our inside man in one of the safe manufacturing companies. It has a devilish combination but a skilled peterman should be able to solve it in five minutes or less. Are you ready for the challenge?'

Harrison took a closer look at the dial. As he did so, he felt his body tense with apprehension. Was he really capable of tackling this? He believed that he was a talented amateur when it came to opening safes, but something special and extra complicated may very well defeat him, and then the fat would truly be in the fire.

'Well,' he said at length, 'I ain't seen one like this before. Is this a trick?'

'Certainly not. No trick, I assure you. It is cunning and difficult, but if you are as talented as you profess, you should be able to release the lock with comparative ease.'

'All right.' Harrison flexed his fingers and licked each one before letting them hover over the combination dial. He knew that most combination locks used a wheel pack, a set of wheels which must be positioned in parallel in order for the safe to be opened. The number of wheels was determined by how many digits there are in the combination. They were usually six digits, which gave the possibility of a million options. Only by sensitive tumbling and attentive hearing might one secure the correct combination to release the lock.

Moran took his watch out of his pocket, unclasped it from its chain and placed it on the table. 'I'll give you five minutes, Mr Harrison. When the second hand reaches twelve you may start.'

Harrison's fingers touched the cold metal and he leaned his ear close to the dial as he began to turn it slowly. At the same time, he tried hard to imagine what six-figure combination Moran had used. Was it purely a random one or had the numbers some special significance? He moved the dial slowly as he held his breath. When he had turned it a full circumference there was nothing. No sound, no registering of a click suggesting a number. This was impossible. No, no, not impossible but baffling. Then he had an idea. He turned the dial in the reverse direction. Still nothing. He bit his lip and glanced at the watch. Almost a minute was up already. Once more he turned the dial in the clockwise direction but very slowly indeed. Then there was a click. It was number two. He allowed himself a tight smile. He repeated the process but yet again there was nothing – no click. Then a thought struck him and he gazed up at the shadowy face of Moran which wore an enigmatic expression.

Harrison turned the dial again in the reverse direction and then clockwise. Sure enough there was another click. Number one this time. Now he afforded himself a small inner smile. He had sussed out the secret process which was turning the dial in reverse to begin with, an action which primed the wheels inside the lock to be accessed when the dial was turned back in the clockwise direction. It was the rhythm of one forward, one back and then one forward again. Repeating this routine another four times, he had secured the combination and the lock sprang open. Harrison wiped a thin sheen of sweat from his brow before glancing at the time on Moran's watch; two minutes, twenty seconds.

Harrison sat back in his chair but said nothing. He subjugated the immense relief he felt and awaited Moran's response. It was clear that the Colonel was surprised, shocked even, at Harrison's acumen.

'That was most impressive,' Moran said and he shot out his hand. 'Welcome aboard. I am sure we will be able to make ample use of you.'

Another hurdle. The track was clear again, thought Harrison, who was almost tempted to touch his forelock but thought better of it. Instead he grasped Moran's hand in a hearty shake.

'What now then?' he asked. 'Where do we go from here?'

Chapter Twenty-nine

In a discreet restaurant just off Whitehall, a man and a woman were ensconced in a private booth, toying with their food while they indulged in deep conversation. The man was Sir Gregory Thornton, one of the junior equerries to the Queen and also a valued member of the Moriarty Organisation – their informant in the establishment. The woman, its new mistress.

'Remind me precisely when the necklace arrives in this country,' she said, her voice low and melodic, 'I need to make sure that there have been no changes since our last contact? Nothing must be left to chance.'

'The ambassador travels from Paris next Tuesday. On arrival in London, it will be announced that the necklace will be held in the main branch of City and Counties bank until the morning of the dinner, before being taken under guard to Buckingham Palace. As you are aware, in reality it will be transported secretly to a small non-descript branch of the bank in Broad Street near Lisson Grove.'

The lady arched her eyebrows in surprise. 'A small branch.'

Sir Gregory nodded. 'It was thought that such a move would fool any felon with a notion of stealing the gaudy trinket. They would be expecting high security. It will be taken there while an empty casket, accompanied by armed officers, will be placed in due formal ceremony in the vaults of the main branch of the bank on the Strand.'

She smiled. 'Very clever of them. Thank you for telling me. With this knowledge it should make my task all the easier.'

'Not quite, my dear. They have installed the latest strongbox from America in the Lisson Grove branch as a precaution. The new one from Finch and Rosenberg. You'll need a pretty good fellow to get into that.'

Sir Gregory's dining companion took a sip of wine and then dabbed her lips with a napkin. 'Allow me to worry about that,' she said smoothly. 'What I require of you are the floor plans of this small branch, including the location of the strong room.'

Sir Gregory beamed and slid his hand into his inside pocket and withdrew a long manila envelope. 'I anticipated your request, my dear. You'll find all the information you require in there.'

'Perspicacious as usual, Sir Gregory. I thank you again.'

'My pleasure. Rest assured I shall inform you if there are any alterations to the arrangements. By Tuesday evening the necklace will be in the safe in the Broad Street branch until the following Saturday morning. You have four nights in which to deal with the matter.'

She gave a gentle chuckle. 'Scotland Yard will be greatly dismayed when they learn that the old Moriarty firm is back in business. In fact I should say apoplectic. It is almost a pity that Sherlock Holmes won't be around to share their discomfort.'

* * *

The following morning after Harrison's test with Colonel Moran, he and Brooks were devouring a fine cooked breakfast prepared by Mrs Doherty.

'The thing is, Harrison, my friend,' said Brooks as he was dipping his bread into the bright yellow of his fried egg, 'Moran's ordered us to leave the Dormitory and set up in our own private quarters in readiness for work.'

'Work?'

Brooks grinned, wiping the yolk that had dribbled on his chin. 'There's a big job coming up and I reckon we're going to be involved.'

'Both of us?'

'Well, me really but you will be one of the troops in the background, no doubt.'

'What sort of big job?'

'Old Moran wasn't saying. He was being very evasive, which is always a sign that it's going to be something special. Obviously, it will involve cracking some crib or other.'

'When?'

Brooks shrugged. 'How do I know? We'll be told when the time is right. You ask too many questions, Mr Nosey Parker. You're with the Organisation now. It's your job to take orders, not ask questions. You'll be put in the picture when they think it appropriate. So relax, chum. Let's find a gaff to lay low and wait. In the meantime we can treat ourselves to a few pints of ale. The mountain will come to Mohammed in due course.'

* * *

Harrison and Brooks ended up in a cheap boarding house in Brixton, each with their own room. The establishment was known grandly as Mrs Slater's Guest House. The proprietor was a sour-faced crone who appeared as decrepit as the property. Harrison knew that in camping down here he was involved in another waiting game, but there were certain things he now had to do. He told Brooks he was going out to find himself 'some decent clobber: I feel such a scruff.'

'Yeah,' came the reply, 'you look like one.' Brooks chortled at his own observation. 'Hey, but be back before six so we can go boozing,' he added.

Once outside, Harrison hailed a cab to take him to Millman Street, near Euston Road. It was here that he had one of the five small refuges in the city where he could change his disguises and become someone else completely. Checking carefully that he had not been followed, once inside the cramped quarters, he dusted off the mirror and stared at the strange face he saw there. Who was this man with the shaved head, thick moustache, straggly beard and the vivid scar on the left cheek (a genuine cut adorned with waterproof make-up of his own devising) along with the row of protruding yellowing teeth? Well, it's me, he thought, although he was well aware that he certainly did not look like Sherlock Holmes at all. 'Thank heavens for that,' he murmured softly as this thought struck him, and he began to dismantle Nigel Harrison, the character he had become. Within twenty minutes, he was gazing at his sleek saturnine features. With a slick dark blonde wig, he was closer to the Holmes of old, apart from the scar and the thick moustache and beard, now neatly trimmed, both of which he longed to shave off. However, these accoutrements to his features had to stay for the time being, for they were needed when he reverted back to his gaol-bird alter ego.

The eyes shone brightly and he smiled with real pleasure to see something close to his old self, in spite of the dreadful hirsute appendages and slightly brassy hair. He chose a shabby tweed suit from a limited wardrobe of items. He completed the outfit with a battered Homburg. He placed his Harrison disguise in a small leather briefcase and left the premises.

Twenty minutes later a cab dropped him at the archway to Scotland Yard. He entered and made his way to the reception desk. A young constable who was scribbling some details down in a record book looked up at his approach.

'Can I be of assistance,' he said mechanically. There was dull boredom in those glassy eyes.

'I wish to see Inspector Lestrade, urgently.'

The constable suddenly perked up and made no attempt to suppress a smile. 'Do you now? Well, I am sure the Inspector is extremely preoccupied on important business so perhaps you should tell me what it's all about.'

Holmes sighed heavily. 'If you wish to remain on the force, I suggest you contact Lestrade's office now and say that "the ghost" needs to see him urgently and things will be sorted. Otherwise, you may find yourself in serious hot water.'

The dark underlying threat of Holmes' words and the mention of the code words 'the ghost' galvanised the now very pale young constable. In less than five minutes Holmes was walking into Inspector Lestrade's office.

The Inspector was sitting at his desk drinking a cup of tea from a large mug, which he almost dropped as the figure of Sherlock Holmes appeared before him.

'Blimey,' he cried, steadying his mug, 'you do look like you belong down the greyhound races in that get up.'

Holmes smiled. 'You should have seen me an hour ago.'

'Take a seat, my friend. Would you care for a mug of tea?'

Holmes shook his head. 'No, I haven't time. I need to be brief and return to my new base. However, there are certain things I need to discuss with you as a matter of urgency. I am here to see you as I am aware that it would be too dangerous to commit details to a letter or telegram, go to Baker Street or attempt to visit the Diogenes Club. I am sure these places are under scrutiny by the Organisation. So, I must use you as my conduit and provide you with information that you need to know and must pass on to my brother and Watson.'

'Very well, I am all ears.'

The interview with Lestrade lasted about fifteen minutes. The inspector did most of the listening while Holmes brought the policeman up to date with events and detailed what he wanted Lestrade to do, with instructions for Mycroft and Watson. Then Holmes requested to visit the washroom in order to return to the persona of Nigel Harrison. The wig was removed, the teeth inserted, the moustache was ruffled. As he emerged in this guise, Lestrade gazed at him open-mouthed. 'Dear Lord, I bet your own mother wouldn't recognise you like that.'

'It's not my mother I am concerned about,' observed Holmes pointedly. 'And now I must go.'

'Rely on me, Mr Holmes, to organise things as you suggested. I'll get two of my best men on the job.'

'Thank you and au revoir.' With a gentle salute, Nigel Harrison left the room and Scotland Yard by the secret rear exit. Very soon he was returning to his new base of operations at Mrs Slater's guest house.

Chapter Thirty

Later that evening, Jacob Brooks came bursting into Harrison's room grinning broadly. 'Are you ready, my friend? Time to visit a tavern and sup a tankard or two, or maybe more.'

Harrison, who was lying on his bed apparently dozing, pulled himself up into a sitting position. 'Ready when you are, squire,' he chirped. 'Let me grab a jacket and we'll be off.'

As the pair left the premises of Mrs Slater's guest house, Harrison noted two loafers hanging about on the pavement on the across the street. As he and Brooks moved down the street, the two men followed casually at a distance.

Good old Lestrade, thought Harrison. It was reassuring to know that he had Mycroft, Watson and the police force behind him.

The pair landed up in a tavern called the Pig and Whistle on Brixton Road. The atmosphere was thick with tobacco smoke and filled mainly with sad-eyed men putting their dreary lives at a distance and out of focus through the medium of alcohol.

Brooks edged his way to the bar with Harrison in tow. After ordering two tankards of ale, they made their way to the corner of the room, securing a couple of seats at a small table.

Harrison was careful to moderate his drinking, claiming to have an upset stomach. Brooks, who had downed a pint of ale within the first five minutes, grinned and announced, 'I hope to drink enough to give me an upset stomach.'

Glancing around the room, Harrison observed that Lestrade's men had followed them into the tavern and were standing idly by the bar.

'Your round, my friend,' cried Brooks, holding up his empty tankard. Harrison trekked to bar and acquired another pint. In doing so, he exchanged covert glances with the two men.

By the time Brooks was on to his fourth pint, his eyes were rolling erratically and his speech was beginning to slur.

'Did you get any idea what kind of job Moran has in store for us?' Harrison asked, hoping that the alcohol would have loosened his associate's tongue.

'Wouldn't you like to know?' he grinned, nodding his head idiotically.

'Well, yes. As I'm going to be involved in some way, it would be nice to be informed what it's all about.'

'You will be told in due course. Even I don't know the full details yet...'

'When will she tell us?'

Brooks thrust his tankard down with force upon the table, some of the brew splashing over the sides. 'There you go again, trying to worm information out of me concerning Miss...' He suddenly stopped short.

'Miss...?' prompted Harrison.

'Never you mind.'

'Will I get to meet her, this mysterious female?'

'It's not for me to say. I very much doubt it. Remember, you're only a bloody minion and an untried one at that. You should be grateful I got you in on this job. Now just forget I ever mentioned her. Understand? Now I suggest you drop the subject.'

'Can't blame a fellow for being curious. I want to know what I'm getting myself into. I don't want to end up back in a bloody cell.'

'Maybe, but you know what curiosity did for the cat. Now get me another drink.'

'Don't you think you've had enough?'

'As it happens, I don't.'

'Well, don't expect me to carry you home.'

By the time Harrison had persuaded Brooks that it was time they made their way back to their diggings, he was very wobbly on his feet and in a serious state of drunkenness. Harrison linked his arm and escorted him to the door of the pub and out into the darkened street. They had not gone more than a few yards when Brooks pulled himself erect. 'I'm going to be sick,' he announced with remarkable clarity.

Swiftly, Harrison led him to a nearby narrow alley where, leaning forwards with his arms pressing against the wall, his head down, Brooks vomited copiously. He stayed in this position for some moments, attempting to control his trembling frame.

'Right, let's go,' he said at length, his voice thick and muted. As they both turned to leave the alley, two figures appeared at the entrance. Without a word they advanced and began the assault. One of the men hit Harrison hard on the chin knocking him to the ground, where he was content to stay, feigning unconsciousness, while the two men turned their attention to Brooks. After a few hard body blows to the midriff, he crashed to the floor. It was then that the bulkier of the two men brought his boot down heavily on Brooks' right hand. The safecracker screamed with pain, the noise echoing in the narrow alley like the cry of a wild animal. The assailant repeated the blow before retreating. Within seconds both men had evaporated into the night.

Harrison waited a few minutes before pulling himself to his feet and attending to his companion. He dragged him up into a sitting position and tapped his face gently in an attempt to bring him round. Slowly the eyes opened and then closed in a wince of pain. 'My hand,' Brooks cried. 'My bloody hand.' He raised it up in front of his face and Harrison could see that it was bloody and mangled, the fingers twisted and limp. Brooks cried out again and it wasn't clear whether it was as result of pain or despair. Harrison concluded that it must be a mixture of the two.

'It's bloody useless. My hand. My hand,' Brooks moaned.

'Come on, let's get back to the diggings and see if we can rig up a dressing.'

'My hand… it's …' He was crying now. Harrison could not help but feel some pity for the man, despite the fact that, from another perspective, the evening had been a great success.

On returning to the guest house, Harrison dressed Brooks' broken hand as best he could. He bathed it and then, tearing a pillowcase into strips, he bound them around the broken, swollen fingers. Brooks sobbed and gibbered through the process but the amount of alcohol he had consumed that night helped to dull the pain to some extent and once the bandaging was complete, he soon drifted off to sleep.

Harrison returned to his own room, a sliver of guilt in his soul. He had destroyed this man's livelihood, criminal though it was. Desperate times call for desperate measures, he told himself with wavering conviction. He slept uneasily that night.

Chapter Thirty-one

❧

Since Sherlock Holmes was no longer in residence at Baker Street, Doctor Watson was in the habit of taking a long walk in the morning. It was an attempt to stave off the strange mixture of nervous tension and boredom which consumed him while he waited for news of Holmes and how the venture was progressing. He was also frustrated because he could not take more of an active role in this affair. He was used to being at Holmes' side even in the most dangerous of cases. But not this time. This time he was relegated to the sidelines.

On this particular morning, returning to Baker Street, he found Mycroft waiting for him. As he entered the sitting room, he saw the large form of Holmes' brother pacing the floor, his face concentrated in thought. Watson's heart skipped a beat. Mycroft rarely made social calls unless there was something of extreme importance to prompt them. He knew that Mycroft's presence here must be connected with Holmes' exploits and probably concerned unforeseen circumstances.

'Ah, Doctor, you've been for a long walk, eh, down along the Embankment.'

'Yes… but?'

'The light-coloured mud adhering to your toe caps and splashes to the bottom of your trouser legs reveals the location. That greyish crumbly mud is quite distinctive to that stretch by the river where the new gas mains are being laid and the fact that the mud is now dry indicates the duration of your walk.'

Watson gave a smile. 'Of course. You have news?'

'Indeed I do. Lestrade has been in touch and informed me that the deed I had co-ordinated was done. Friend Brooks will never crack a safe again.'

'Holmes is unharmed?'

'Possibly a sore chin, nothing more.'

'So we move on to the next stage.'

'In essence,' mused Mycroft, 'although we, including Sherlock, have no real power to move on, to direct events. We have prepared the ground, but it is our enemies who must now take the initiative.'

'And if they don't…'

Mycroft pursed his lips and frowned. 'Then,' he muttered gloomily, 'Sherlock will be in a very sticky situation indeed.'

Jacob Brooks stayed in bed for two days after the attack, nursing his shattered hand. He sipped whisky and drank a sedative mixture that Harrison had managed to secure from an apothecary he had located a few streets way.

'You've got to get a message to the Colonel. He's got to know about this.' He held up the bloodied bandage that covered his right hand. 'He's been relying on me – now I'm downright useless. But if

I don't let him know it could be worse for me. He don't like being kept in the dark, the Colonel don't.'

'How do I get in touch with him?'

'I'll dictate a note. You write it. I'll tell him what happened and hope he'll be sympathetic. I may not be able to tackle a safe again, but I have my other uses.'

'How will I pass the note to him? Do you have an address?'

Brooks smiled. It was the first time since the assault. Faint amusement seemed alien on those gaunt and haggard features. 'Don't be stupid. Very few know where he hangs out. You must take the note to the Dormitory and Irish will see that the Colonel gets it.'

Harrison did as he was bidden. He wrote the note, dictated in a halting fashion by Brooks. The paper was then folded over and sealed with candle wax.

'I'll take it to the Dormitory straight away,' said Harrison, slipping the missive into his inner jacket pocket. 'Think he'll be sympathetic?'

'Not particularly, but the Colonel would react badly if I don't let on that I can't assist him in this new project.'

'What about the leader of the Organisation?'

Brooks gave a snort of derision. 'If anything she has a colder heart than her father.'

At this statement, Harrison felt an icy hand grasp his heart and for a few moments he could hardly breathe. Had he really heard what he thought Brooks had said: 'she has a colder heart than her father.' Electricity surged through his system as he digested this statement. It was further confirmation of what he and Mycroft had come to believe: that this woman had the strongest of connections with Professor James Moriarty. All the disparate elements, the paid education at a French establishment, the nefarious activities of Madame Defarge, who had mysteriously disappeared, and the emergence of a young woman taking a major role in the Professor's old Organisation now made sense. Harrison had suspected it but Brooks had unwittingly provided the final piece of the puzzle. It was a fantastic revelation but it fitted all the facts perfectly. Who else could she be? Crime in the blood is liable to take the strangest forms.

He needed to know more but he was aware that if he attempted to question Brooks further, he could clam up immediately. He had made the statement without thinking. In his tired, distressed state he had let slip this terrible secret, but Harrison knew that he certainly would not be prepared to say more. Accepting this fact, he did not react. He simply rose from the bedside and headed for the door. 'I'll go now and deliver the note.'

Brooks simply nodded and then lay back on his pillow.

On his journey to the Dormitory, Harrison considered in detail the information he had just acquired – that the woman who was heading the Organisation was almost certainly Professor James Moriarty's daughter. Why had she arrived on the scene now? He realised these were questions he could not answer without further data, but it struck him that her presence did explain why he had been a target for torment and destruction. It was her revenge for his being responsible for her father's death. The Professor was indeed, dead, but the vendetta continued. His whole body tingled with excitement as he realised that it would not be too long before he was able to meet this mysterious woman – his cunning bête noire.

Chapter Thirty-two

Cordelia Moriarty held a magnifying glass over the plans of the bank premises of the City and Counties branch on Broad Street, which had been provided by Sir Gregory Thornton. She was intent on familiarising herself with every detail of the layout. Things were going very smoothly with the preparations for the robbery, but she was well aware that it would be dangerous to relax or take anything for granted. She needed to know the place by heart.

There was a gentle knock on the door. It had a recognisable staccato rhythm. She waited a moment and the knock came again as she anticipated. 'Come in,' she called and Colonel Sebastian Moran entered. She read his features in an instant.

'You look serious,' she said. 'Is something wrong?'

'I'm afraid so.'

'Explain.'

'It's Jacob Brooks...'

'He's not been apprehended?'

'No, it is worse than that. He was drunk and attacked by a couple of roughs who beat him up and damaged his hand. His right hand.'

'His safecracking hand?'

Moran nodded.

'How badly?'

'He sent me a note. He says it is now useless. He will not be able to help us with the robbery.'

Cordelia Moriarty gave a heavy sigh. 'Damn! I thought things were going too smoothly. We have already installed our man, Ralph Cousins, as the night watchman and I have the plans of the building. Now this...'

'Perhaps all is not lost. There is that cove who got out of gaol with Brooks. He is a nifty fellow with his fingers.'

'Safecracking?'

'Yes, I gave him our special trial model and he cracked it in just over two minutes.'

'Did he?'

'To be honest, it struck me that he was just as good as Brooks, if not better.'

Cordelia Moriarty's eyes flashed with interest. 'Can he be trusted?'

'His background checks out, and obviously, he hasn't been put to the test, but according to Brooks it was his scheme that got them out of prison. He's obviously a bright spark.'

'You say he was very skilful with the trial device.'

'Yes. I was impressed.'

'Then perhaps we will have to trust him. However, I want to see him first, judge him for myself. Bring him here so I can get the measure of the man, and have him followed from now on until the job is completed satisfactorily. If there's a hint of anything suspicious, you know what to do.'

Moran gave a gentle bow. 'Your wish is my command.'

'It had better be,' responded Cordelia Moriarty without humour before returning her attention to the plans on her desk.

Jacob Brooks had taken to drowning his despair in alcohol. The prospect of the permanent loss of flexibility in his right hand and with it the means to earn an illicit living by breaking into safes had hit him hard. He had taken to not rising from his bed until the afternoon and then spending enough time in a tavern to get himself drunk before heading back to his sack. Harrison, while keeping an eye on him, made no effort to alter his behaviour. He knew this would end up with raised voices and anger. Moran had not been in touch in response to the note and both men were waiting nervously for this to occur.

Two days after the message had been delivered, Harrison decided to visit the Dormitory to ascertain that it had in fact been passed on to Colonel Moran. It was dark when he left the guest house and made his way down the street. As he did so, out of the evening gloom, a black carriage with two horses drew up alongside the kerb some six feet ahead of him. It was a four-wheeler with windows of dark frosted glass. As he passed the carriage, the door swung open and a voice boomed out from the interior, 'Get in, Mr Harrison.'

Harrison recognised that dark voice and clipped military tones. It was Colonel Moran. He smiled to himself. It looked like the call had come at last. He turned swiftly and, without a word, climbed aboard the cab. Moran sat in the shadows at the far side. 'Good evening,' he said as he tapped the roof with his cane and the carriage set off.

'What's this all about?'

'You'll have to be patient.'

'Well, at least you could tell me where we are going.'

Moran pursed his lips in amusement. 'I could, but I have no intention of doing so.'

Harrison glanced at the dark frosted windows that blanked his vision of the outside world. There was no way he would be able to see the route that was being taken. His knowledge of London and its thoroughfares was prodigious and by keeping a sharp ear to the sounds beyond the cab and noting each twist and turn of the vehicle as it travelled to its destination, initially he had a clear idea of the route. However, several times the carriage suddenly changed directions and it struck Harrison that it was almost certainly driving in circles to confuse him, in order to prevent his identifying the location of their destination and the length of the journey. Most of the time the wheels seemed to be turning over smooth asphalt but occasionally there would be a juddering rattle as the carriage passed over a paved causeway or a cobbled lane. According to his watch the journey lasted just under an hour. He realised that they may have travelled quite a distance from Brixton or but a few short miles. Eventually, the carriage came to a shuddering halt and Moran leant across and opened the door.

'Time to get out, Mr Harrison,' he said. 'We will go straight into the house. Do not linger.'

As surreptitiously as he could, Harrison took stock of his surroundings. In the darkness, he glimpsed a massive, uninviting house, the façade draped with ivy and fronted by a pillared portico. It was on one of the pillars that he observed something that gladdened his heart and was stored away in his memory for future use.

Beyond the portico a door stood ajar as though in readiness for their arrival. He was quickly ushered into the hall by Moran, who closed the door hard behind them, its boom echoing down the long gloomy corridors.

'This way.' Moran had taken up a lamp and led Harrison down a gloomy oak panelled passageway until they came to a door at the far end. 'This is where I leave you for the moment. Go inside.' Without another word he retreated down the corridor, taking the wavering lamp with him.

Harrison passed through the door and found himself in a library with a log fire burning in a marble fireplace and large candles arranged on the mantel. A substantial oak desk with a walnut veneer was situated close to a tall, arched stained glass window with intricate designs, and a pair of winged armchairs were placed either side of the fireplace. Two walls housed bookshelves from floor to ceiling, many of which were ancient tomes; a number, Harrison observed, dealt with mathematical theory. A small table in the corner housed a collection of decanters and a gasogene. Noting the architecture of the room, the cornices and the shape of the fireplace, he determined that the house was of the Jacobean period, tallying with Mycroft's description of the place he had been held prisoner.

He was just about to sit down in one of the winged armchairs when the door opened and a tall, slim figure entered. It was a young woman, dressed in a closely fitted black dress. She had pale features, high cheekbones and bright blue eyes. Her long dark hair hung down, curling around her chin. For a moment Harrison was mesmerised by this vision. Was this in fact the daughter of the Napoleon of Crime, Professor James Moriarty? Was there anything about her features that hinted at her dark inheritance? He could see none apart – perhaps – for the slight nodding of the head.

She gave him a calm, mechanical smile that was pleasant enough, but it held no warmth. 'I observe that you were about to take a seat, Mr Harrison. Pray do so.'

'Thank you, Miss...?'

She glared at him coldly.

'You have me at a disadvantage. You know my name, and who I am, but I have no knowledge of you...'

Her smile broadened. 'Having an advantage... that is always how I play my game.'

'I am not sure what you mean.'

'Suffice it to say that I am in control.'

'In control of...?'

'The Organisation. You.'

'Me? I like to think I am in control of me.'

'The usual misapprehension. Would you care for a drink?'

'Very civilised.'

'What is your poison?'

'A whisky and soda would be fine.'

'I will join you,' she murmured and glided to the drinks table and prepared the libations.

After handing Harrison his drink she sat opposite him. 'Colonel Moran seems impressed with your skills in cracking open safes.'

Harrison raised his right hand and wriggled his fingers. 'That's nice to know,' he said.

'You are familiar with the monsters produced by Finch and Rosenberg?'

'Indeed I am. Cracked a few in my time.'

'But you will not have encountered their latest model, which they claim will fox the cleverest would-be thief.'

'A wise man once said, "Any puzzle the mind of man has

conceived can be solved by the mind of another".'

The mysterious young woman narrowed her eyes. 'A confident fellow, aren't we?'

'I like to think I have reasons to be so.'

I have researched your background and...' She paused.

Harrison's features remained neutral, but his stomach tensed as he hoped that Mycroft had lived up to his reputation for creative, plausible forgery of lives, records, papers and witnesses.

She continued, 'And I found it satisfactory.'

Harrison's breathing relaxed a little. He smiled and replied, 'A villain always leaves his tracks, however hard he tries to erase them.'

'An interesting childhood. The son of a clockmaker.'

'That's how I became interested in mechanical workings and developed my skill with these.' Harrison held up his hands.

'You certainly impressed Colonel Moran and I trust his opinions implicitly, but you are here tonight so that I can get my own measure of you. We have you in mind for a very special job. Your comrade Jacob Brooks was due to do it but as he is now... incapacitated, it seems that you are our ideal substitute.'

'That suits me fine. What's it all about?'

'You do not need to know all the details, only the aspects of the matter that relate to you. Let us say that a precious item is locked away in one of Finch and Rosenberg's super safes in a small branch of the City and Counties bank and we need to retrieve it.'

'How will I gain entry to the bank to get to the safe?'

'That has all been arranged. We have planted one of our men in the bank as night watchman. On the night of the robbery he will make sure that the door at the rear of the premises is unlocked. You will be able to slip inside with ease. Your main task is to open the safe and extract the item we require.'

'And what is this "item"?'

The young woman paused. 'It is a necklace. That's all you need to know.'

'Must be a pretty special necklace.'

'It is a necklace, that is all you need to know.'

From her intransigent tone Harrison knew he had to leave the subject there. She was obviously not going to reveal any further details and if he pressed her for more information it may well arouse her suspicions. However, he had a pretty good idea concerning the identity of the necklace.

'And what do I get for my services?'

'You will be amply rewarded. But, beware, you must not fail me.' She paused and gave him a penetrating look. 'So then, I assume that you are prepared to join us and assist in this venture.'

'You have gauged the measure of me?'

She hooded her eyes. It was a cold and cruel gesture but she did not reply to his question. Instead she said: 'I repeat, I assume you are prepared to accept the challenge?'

Harrison was certain that if he had refused the offer he would not have left the building alive. Although the woman had revealed only the sketchiest of details regarding her plans, giving him the location of the proposed deed was enough to prove fatal to the venture if the information came to the attention of the authorities. Of course, he had no intention of refusing – this was exactly the scenario he had been planning for. He gave a sharp salute. 'I'm on board and reporting for duty, ma'am,' he said.

'Very good.' She rose from her chair and moved to the large desk near the window. 'I think we have concluded tonight's business. Time for you to leave.'

She had that cold, commanding nature that to Harrison was so reminiscent of her father.

'I'd rather know who I was working for. You still haven't told me who you are.'

'And I said that it was time for you to leave,' came the icy reply.

'I see,' he said in resignation, rising from the chair. 'What happens next?'

The mysterious young woman pointed to the door by which he had entered to room, 'Make your way down the corridor and through the main door and you will find the carriage waiting to take you back to your lodgings.'

There was an awkward pause and then she smiled. 'Today is Friday. The robbery is planned for Tuesday night. At nine o'clock on Monday morning a carriage will be waiting outside your berth to bring you here, where you will stay until this particular venture is complete. But take note, Mr Harrison, nothing you do or say between now and then, not even your breathing out or breathing in will go unnoticed. I am not letting you out of my clutches until you have proved yourself worthy of our trust, Mr Harrison. On Monday we will study the plans of the bank together and you will be informed of the various detailed arrangements involved in this interesting business. Is that clear?'

'It is.'

'Then I will bid you goodnight.' She thrust her arm out towards the door. Harrison bowed his head and departed. The carriage was waiting for him, the horses impatiently stomping the ground, their eager breath emitting small clouds of mist into the cool night air. There was no Colonel Moran this time; he was the solitary passenger. As soon as he climbed into the carriage it set off at speed.

On the journey, he reviewed the encounter with the woman

he believed to be Moriarty's daughter. He began recalling the experience in detail in order to extract as much information as he could. She was in her early thirties. Her long elegant fingers and finely marked features held something of the Professor's, whose cold eyes he had seen at close quarters with such a look of hatred in them that it chilled him to think of it, even now. There was a trace of an accent in the voice. It seemed probable that the news of Sherlock Holmes' resurrection from the dead had prompted her to return to England. It was possible that she had been driven by a determination to destroy the man who had been responsible for the death of her father, and as an extra triumph, to resurrect his old Organisation as a tribute to him. To Harrison this theory seemed a logical assessment of the scenario. No doubt she had already overseen some comparatively minor felonies and been responsible for the increasing rate of crime in the city, observed by Mycroft, but this robbery was to be her first major triumph, one that would announce to the authorities and the world at large that the Moriarty firm was in business again. Harrison smiled at his concept and then his smile broadened even further at the thought that in preparing for this major crime she had employed the man she most hated in the world. The man she thought was dead.

There were still many questions to be answered, but the climax to this dark business was imminent and he knew it would place him on his mettle. There was danger ahead, but this did not dishearten him. On the contrary, he was thrilled at the prospect and was determined to rise to the challenge.

When he was dropped off at his lodgings, he noted a rough-looking fellow across the street standing in a doorway, smoking a clay pipe. Obviously one of the Organisation's men keeping a watch on the premises or, to be more precise, on him and his comings and goings.

Once inside, Harrison made his way through the building to the rear and exited into the back yard. Here he scrambled over the wall and made his way by a circuitous route to the main thoroughfare, thus avoiding being seen by Moriarty's sentry. He secured a cab a few streets away and headed off to an address just off the Marylebone Road.

Asking the cabby to wait, he approached a rather shabby looking terrace house, which was all in darkness. He knocked loudly on the door. At length there were sounds of activity within and then the door opened to reveal a short burly woman in a dressing robe brandishing a poker. She peered out at Harrison.

'Who the hell are you and what do you want, knockin' honest folk up at this time of the night?'

'My apologies for calling at such a late hour but the matter is urgent. It's Sherlock Holmes.'

'Sherlock Holmes? You look nothing like Sherlock Holmes.'

'I am in disguise, but it really is me. I need to see your son, Wiggins.'

'What is it, Ma?' came a voice from behind the woman.

'There's a geezer here who claims he's that Sherlock Holmes, him that you do a few jobs for.'

Wiggins squeezed in beside his mother and stared out at the visitor.

'It really is me, Wiggins,' Harrison said with a grin.

'Blimey, it is an' all. I don't know the face but I recognise the voice. You're on a case, then.'

Harrison smiled and nodded. 'I'm always on a case, Wiggins. I need your help with a little errand.'

Wiggins grinned. 'Of course, Mr Holmes. Happy to oblige.'

Chapter Thirty-three

From the journal of John H. Watson

I have always been a light sleeper. This, I suppose, was partly due to my military training when one was expected to be out of bed and dressed very quickly, prepared for whatever was demanded of you. Also, my time with Sherlock Holmes had taught me to be ready on the instant if there was a possibility that danger threatened. However, I had never exactly suffered from insomnia until that period when Holmes left Baker Street with his plan to infiltrate the new Moriarty Organisation. I was unable to rest contentedly not knowing how my friend was faring in his endeavours. Mycroft, Lestrade and I had acquired small crumbs of information, largely from Mycroft's enviable networks. Rather like the late but unlamented Professor, Holmes' brother had a brain of the first order. Like his current antagonist, Mycroft sits, motionless, like a spider in the centre of his own web, but that web has a thousand radiations, and he knows well every quiver of each one of them. However, we lacked detailed knowledge of exactly how my friend's machinations, orchestrated by Mycroft and, to some lesser extent, myself and Lestrade, were progressing.

So it was that I was lying sleepless, staring at the ceiling, wondering how Holmes was coping and when the climax would come. I knew that his actions had placed him in imminent danger of discovery and the resultant loss of his life. It pained me to contemplate such a scenario and I was just about to throw back the covers and head for the sitting room to have a smoke and a hot drink when I heard the tinkling of the doorbell downstairs. My heart skipped a beat. I assumed that a caller at this time of night could only mean one thing: something to do with Holmes and this dark affair.

Hurriedly, I donned a dressing gown and raced down the stairs just in time to see Mrs Hudson emerge from her quarters, a candle in one hand.

'Don't concern yourself, Mrs Hudson,' I said kindly, not wanting to alarm her. 'The caller will have some business with me, no doubt, concerning one of Mr Holmes' cases.'

She gave a sleepy nod of the head and retreated.

Unlocking the door and opening it, I discovered young Wiggins, the leader of the Baker Street Irregulars, standing before me, a cheery grin on his face. He touched his cap in genial salute. 'Evenin' Dr Watson, or should I say mornin'.'

'What brings you here?' I asked, ignoring that particular conundrum.

'I have a message from Mr Holmes.'

'Have you, by Jove,' I said with some excitement.

'Here, he's written it down.' He extracted a sheet of notepaper from his back pocket and handed it to me. I read it eagerly, recognising the easy flow of Holmes' handwriting:

Watson

The end is near. I need a meeting with you, Mycroft and Lestrade. Please get in touch with them and arrange for a rendezvous in the Gloucester Room at the Diogenes Club at noon tomorrow when I will advise of the current situation. Alert Mycroft I will arrive in disguise as Maurice Verne, a city banker.

SH

I thanked Wiggins for the message, passed him a coin for his trouble and hurried upstairs to our sitting room. I poured myself a generous measure of whisky and read the note again. 'The end is near' – my goodness. What on earth, I wondered, were we going to learn tomorrow? Numerous scenarios raced through my brain to no avail. One thing was for sure, I certainly wasn't going to get any sleep tonight.

Chapter Thirty-four

~

After Harrison had visited Wiggins, he travelled to his refuge on Millman Street. Here he changed clothes and his disguise, emerging half an hour later as Maurice Verne, a city banker with tailcoat and striped trousers. His Harrison costume and false teeth were stowed in a capacious carpet bag. Arriving back at his diggings, the sentry across the road, still there, still smoking, raised no interest in this smartly dressed fellow as he made his way into the guest house.

The following morning, having returned to his Harrison persona, he visited Brooks' room. He wasn't there and neither were any of his belongings. His bed had been stripped as though it was ready for a new lodger. Harrison enquired of the landlady regarding Brooks.

'Oh, he's gone. Two gentlemen came to see him last night and he went off with them. Must say he didn't seem too happy about it, but the men paid me for another week's rent to make up for his sudden departure like. He didn't tell you he was going then?'

Harrison shook his head. 'I didn't think he'd leave so quickly,' he said and returned to his room. What, he wondered, was Brooks' fate? Obviously the 'two gentlemen' were members of the Organisation. Harrison grimaced at the thought of what was behind their visit. He had little doubt concerning their intentions. Now that Brooks was of no use as a specialist to them and that he knew too much about the big safecracking operation, he probably was, in the phrase used by the underworld, surplus to requirements.

It was in the persona of Maurice Verne that he left the guest house later that morning. The watcher across the road was a different fellow, but clearly on the lookout for Harrison. Little did he know that in fact Harrison currently resided in a large carpet bag under the floorboards in one of the bedrooms in the guest house.

It was nearing the hour of twelve o'clock when Verne mounted the steps of the Diogenes Club. He announced his name to the commissionaire, saying that he was attending a meeting in the Gloucester Room. The commissionaire had been informed to expect such an individual and summoned a young lackey to convey him to the private chamber. He tapped gently on the door and entered.

It was a small windowless room with a round table in the centre at which were seated three men who rose in unison as Verne entered. They stared nonplussed for a moment at this stranger with the pince-nez and business suit and then Watson laughed. 'Maurice Verne, I presume,' he said moving forward and grabbing the man by the hand and shaking it vigorously.

'For the moment,' came the reply.

'Blimey, Mr Holmes, you are a bleedin' chameleon'. You look nothing like your old self,' observed Lestrade.

'That was his intention. He's always been keen at dressing up to fool people, haven't you, Sherlock, old boy?' remarked Mycroft, patting his brother on the arm.

'Only as a necessity. Now shall we get down to business, I have a great deal to tell you.' Holmes took a seat at the table and in precise economical detail, he regaled his listeners with all that had happened to him since he had taken up residence at Mrs Slater's lodgings.

'The house you were taken to – have you any idea where it is located?' asked Watson.

Holmes shook his head. 'I am sure that the length of carriage ride was a ruse to confuse me, but I can tell you that the building is Jacobean in style – no doubt the same as the place where you spent some time, dear brother, and I observed the name of the place carved into one of the columns by the front door. The lettering was faint, a victim of the time and weather, but nevertheless I was able to make out the words "Pelham House". It should be quite easy to locate the building by researching that name. Had I access to my files at Baker Street it would have been a simple task to identify it.'

'Excellent,' said Mycroft, making a note in his pocketbook.

'Also,' added Holmes, 'the Dormitory is located near Blackfriars Bridge on the south bank. From the outside it appears as a derelict warehouse – with the name Beaumont painted on the wall in faded lettering. I learned that Irish, the man in charge of the place, keeps a ledger with the contact details of all members of the syndicate. The ledger is disguised as business accounts for a small company selling specialist ironmongery to the art trade and indeed, there is a quantity of nails, security screws, picture hooks and cords and packing materials in a semi-functioning store room to add to the illusion of a legitimate business.'

'This is all very useful information,' said Lestrade, rubbing his hands with enthusiasm. 'And you believe that this young woman is really the daughter of Professor Moriarty?'

'I believe so. She certainly has his cunning and criminal acumen. Whether she is actually the spawn of Moriarty is as yet to be proved.'

'Well, Sherlock,' said Mycroft, stroking his chin, 'it is clear that the object of the robbery is obviously the Josephine Necklace which arrives in this country on Monday. My research reveals that it is the only diadem locked away in a London bank of such great value and significance, and therefore the likely lure for the Moriarty gang.'

'I am sure you are right,' agreed Holmes. 'Snatching the priceless gem away, causing embarrassment to the British – and indeed the French government, not to mention the Queen – would bring extra kudos to the gang, establishing them as a force to be reckoned with.'

'Indeed, Mr Holmes,' said Lestrade solemnly. 'That's why they have to be stopped.'

Mycroft nodded. 'It is a consummation devoutly to be wished. The necklace is to be lodged secretly in a modest bank premises, as an extra precaution against theft.'

Holmes nodded. 'That would be the Broad Street Branch out at Lisson Grove way.'

Mycroft raised an eyebrow. 'How on earth do you know that?'

'It is the only bank that has just installed a Finch and Rosenberg, the latest wunderkind strongbox from America. I keep up to date with such matters, dear brother.'

'Apparently.'

'Unfortunately, the exact details of the robbery have not yet been vouchsafed to me. I can tell you that the proposed date is Tuesday next. However, their plan of operation will only be revealed to me when I am taken back to Pelham House on Monday. I will be kept there until the robbery is due to take place and therefore that means I will have no opportunity of communicating with you. It is already risky as my current lodgings are being watched – though I have to say, not very effectively. What I do know is that the Organisation has their man employed as the night watchman who will facilitate my entry to the bank. My main problem is that brute of a safe. It is very much an unknown quantity. While I am competent in cracking run of the mill items, it is quite possible that this monster could defeat me. This must not happen, so, Mycroft, I have to ask you to arrange for the lock to be neutralised in some fashion so that I can open it with ease.'

Mycroft gave his brother a stern look. 'I have no doubt it can be arranged but it makes the contents extremely vulnerable.'

'Indeed, that is the object of the exercise. I am supposed to steal the necklace after all. Once it has been taken and handed over to Milady, then Lestrade and his men can pounce, and she and the rest of her felonious tribe can be hauled away.'

'Why must we wait for this, Holmes?' asked Watson. 'Why can't we just arrest the devils now?'

'On what evidence? There is yet not enough proof to convict anyone apart from Colonel Moran. The others don't really matter, just a group of criminal foot soldiers. It is the head spider we need. Without her presence, the rest of the Organisation will be rudderless. It is she who is the real threat, the dangerous corrupting influence. She must be stopped.'

Holmes spoke with passion, his eyes flashing fiercely and a faint blush blooming on his cheeks.

'So what do you suggest, Mr Holmes?' asked Lestrade.

'As you all will appreciate, this matter is a most delicate one.

There are no certainties and we all may have to be prepared to improvise as the events dictate, but I will lay out my plans and suggest the help that you can provide in order to bring a successful conclusion to this venture.'

'Very well, Mr Holmes, go ahead…'

Chapter Thirty-five

By Monday, Harrison was installed in an attic room at Pelham House. He had been collected by Colonel Moran from Mrs Slater's guest house at nine o'clock, as instructed. On the journey Harrison had attempted to find out what had happened to Jacob Brooks, but the Colonel remained resolutely silent, smoking his cigar and behaving as though he was the only passenger in the carriage.

On arrival at the house, the Colonel disappeared, and Harrison was passed into the charge of a tall, muscular fellow of dour demeanour whom Harrison assumed took on the role of butler or bodyguard. He did not give his name and hardly spoke, merely communicated by means of grunted gestures. Harrison followed the man up three flights of stairs to a small bedroom which held a single bed, a chair, a sink and an ancient chest of drawers. Once inside, his guide retreated, and he was left alone. He heard the key turning in the lock. Sure enough, as he tried the handle, he knew he was a prisoner. He shrugged his shoulders. It was what he had expected. As he lay down on the bed, he felt somewhat exhilarated at the contemplation of the challenge that awaited him. However cautious this cunning female and her cohorts were about him, he knew they had placed a great deal of reliance on his expertise and function in this particular assignment.

As the evening shadows invaded the room by means of the skylight, he heard the door unlocking. Within seconds it was open and the sour-faced butler was standing on the threshold. He thrust out his arm, beckoning Harrison forward. 'Come,' he said in guttural tones. He was led down the stairs to the room he had been to on his first visit to the house. The woman he had met before was seated at her desk, studying a large sheet of paper laid out on the surface which Harrison determined were the floor plans of a building. No doubt it was the Broad Street premises of the City and Counties bank.

'I trust you've had a rest after your journey,' she said, without looking up.

'Yes, but I was not too happy to be locked in.'

'Simple precautions, that's all. You are untested metal after all. Now cast aside your petulance and come and study this floor plan. You will need to know it intimately before tomorrow night.'

Harrison did as he was bidden. The branch indeed was a small one. On the ground floor there was an office for the manager, a small general office, the counter section and a strong room. Behind the counter space was a small washroom, a kitchen area and lavatory. Beyond was a porch and the rear entrance to the property, which was accessed from a narrow lane. The two large upstairs rooms appeared to have no designated use, but the new safe was in the basement, which was situated towards the rear of the building.

She hovered over the plans, indicating the various sections to Harrison. On the third finger of her right hand, she wore a bright ruby ring which sparked brightly in the dim light. 'The basement is accessed through the manager's office. There is a false bookcase there which provides access to a set of stairs leading down. However, you will make your entry to the premises by the rear door, which conveniently is on a level with the basement. This will be unlocked by our night watchman. All you have to do…'

'…is break open the monster in the basement?'

She smiled. 'Exactly.'

Harrison studied the document for a few minutes in silence. 'I've got it,' he said at length, tapping his temple. 'It's in here, safe and sound.'

'Good, then we shall go through and dine.'

The dining room, which was situated next door was a dark panelled room with an impressive stone fireplace which housed a roaring log fire. The room was dominated by substantial oak table which was set for two diners. The room was candlelit with one large silver candelabra placed at the centre of the table.

'Take a seat,' she said cordially, indicating the one to the left of the table, while she placed herself at the head.

The oafish butler materialised out of the shadows at the far end of the room. 'We will dine now, Bassick. Pour the wine and then you can serve the food.'

He grunted his understanding of her wishes. After he had dealt with the wine, he disappeared through a door at the far end of the room.

'The Colonel will not be dining with us?' asked Harrison.

His hostess shook her head. 'He has business elsewhere.'

Harrison raised his glass. 'Your good health.'

'And yours,' came the reply which held a dark undertone.

She was, thought Harrison, a striking woman. Not conventionally beautiful but her face had a pleasing aspect to it and her eyes were remarkable, a deep blue with a glistening sheen that seemed to hold one's attention. Her voice, husky and mellifluous with that attractive trace of a foreign accent was pleasing on the ear. He rarely thought of women in terms of attractiveness. Indeed, the thought of any kind of romantic attraction was abhorrent to him, but nevertheless, he could see how a man could easily fall for the charms of this creature. He remembered well the appeal of the American adventuress, Irene Adler, and he saw that there were similarities between the two women. They both possessed alluring beauty but with cunning minds as sharp as a guillotine.

'Now we know each other better, perhaps you would care to tell me who you are,' he said gently as though passing an innocent comment on the weather. He knew he could make such a bold comment as he was well aware that he was the key instrument in her plans and without him it would not succeed.

'Oh, Mr Harrison, I believe you already know.' She smiled, stroking her cheek casually, the ruby ring appearing as a droplet of blood sliding down the smooth flesh.

'I may have hazarded a guess, but it may be that arrow fell short of the bull's eye.'

'Tell me your guess.'

'You are some relation of the late lamented Professor Moriarty. Perhaps his daughter?'

'Bull's eye. Your aim is accurate. Yes, I am Cordelia Moriarty and the Professor was my father.'

His expression remained neutral, with just a hint of admiration, though internally the final confirmation caused his stomach to lurch. His darkest intimations and deductions had had been correct. The innate criminal malevolence of Professor Moriarty survived in this evil and cunning offspring. It was the stuff of nightmares. It was only with a great effort that he managed to maintain his Harrison persona.

'I hardly knew him,' she continued, seemingly unaware of the effect her admission had wrought on her dinner guest, 'for he sent me away to France when I was but an infant. However, he maintained my living there. I returned to this country with the intention of supporting him. We had only a brief reconciliation before his tragic death at the hands of Sherlock Holmes. I mourned for quite some months and bided my time as I prepared myself to resurrect my father's Organisation. With the help of Colonel Moran, I was in the process of setting a structure in place when we received the news that Sherlock Holmes had escaped death at the Reichenbach Falls, and that he had returned to London, involving himself in detective work once more. This really upset my applecart for a while, as you might imagine.'

She paused and took a sip of wine. 'It was a cruel stroke of fate. His murderer was still alive. It made my father's death even more of a tragedy.'

'But the fellow Holmes is dead now. I read of his funeral.'

'Oh, yes. Where my father failed, I succeeded in destroying that demon.'

'You...'

'Yes, me! I was responsible for Sherlock Holmes' death – a real one this time. Now I am free of any restraint that he may have caused me and that is why I am after the Josephine Necklace. Not purely for any monetary value – although that will be useful. However, the main purpose of this robbery is to establish to Scotland Yard and all law enforcement authorities that the Moriarty firm is back in business and big business.'

'That is remarkable,' observed Harrison with enthusiasm. 'I feel privileged to be part of the scheme.'

'If you perform your duties well tomorrow night, you will be rewarded appropriately.'

'I will not fail you.'

'I will be there to see that you don't.'

Harrison paused, his eyes widening in surprise. 'You... you will be there?' This was a shock to him. He had assumed that she would keep her distance.

'Naturally. On this occasion, I intend to be present at the moment of triumph when you lift that necklace from the safe, as the Organisation moves to the next level. But, my dear Harrison, I shall also be in attendance in order to make sure that you do not abscond with the necklace to feather your own nest.'

'I assure you...'

'Oh, I am certain that you do and I have a tendency to believe you, but I didn't get where I am by allowing any risks, however small, to upset my plans.'

'The proof is in the pudding, eh?'

'Precisely.'

Following the meal, Cordelia Moriarty bid Harrison an early good night. 'You need a deep and refreshing sleep in order to be bright and both physically and intellectually agile for the rigours of tomorrow.'

Of that there was no doubt, thought Harrison as he made his way to his eyrie at the top of the house. Bassick was but a few steps behind him. Once inside the room, the door was locked again.

Harrison sat on the bed and heaved a sigh. It had been a remarkable evening and a strenuous one. At times it had been difficult to keep in character, maintaining the appropriate reactions to what he had learned. This Moriarty woman was indeed a fascinating creature with a ferocity of purpose which was both impressive and chilling. He could not help but admire her while at the same time renewing his determination to bring her to justice and destroy her Organisation. The fact that she intended to be with him when he opened the safe was a surprise, but on consideration it was fitting that she would be apprehended at the scene of the crime rather than later. He was confident that Mycroft and Lestrade would follow his instructions in preparation for the robbery the following night. No doubt they would have also discovered the location of Pelham Lodge and already have it under surveillance.

As the hour crept past midnight, he lay on the bed, his whole body tingling with apprehension. Tomorrow would bring the climax of all the weeks of waiting and dissembling. He hoped that fate would allow the dice to fall in his favour.

Finale

Chapter Thirty-six

It was late afternoon, and already Samuel Wilkins was slipping on his overcoat in readiness to make the journey to the Broad Street branch of the City and Counties bank when there came a knock at the front door of his tiny, terraced cottage. He stiffened with apprehension. He never had visitors. And he certainly did not want one today, not now. He reached into his coat pocket and withdrew a pistol. The knock came again, more insistent this time.

Wilkins leaned against the door. 'Who is it?' he called in his throaty asthmatic voice.

'Moran,' responded the voice from outside.

Wilkins hurriedly opened the door and let his visitor in.

'Sorry, Colonel, I wasn't expecting you.'

Moran said nothing for a while as he moved further into the house.

'Is something up? Is the job off?'

Moran shook his head. 'No, but there has been a change of plan.'

* * *

Some hours later as day was moving to evening, Colonel Sebastian Moran approached the rear of the bank. It was reached by traversing a narrow alley which ran parallel to the main thoroughfare. There was a large iron gate protecting the yard and the back entrance itself. He unlocked the gate, passed through and locked it again. Stealthily he made his way to the rear entrance to the premises, but just as he was about to slip the key into the lock, he felt something cold and hard press on the nape of his neck. He was experienced enough to realise that it was the barrel of a revolver.

'This is where your story ends, Colonel,' said a voice softly in his ear. It was a voice he knew all too well.

Bassick collected Harrison from his room as dusk was falling and led him to the entrance of the house, where a carriage was waiting. Without a word, Bassick indicated that he should enter before the butler clambered into the driving seat. Cordelia Moriarty was waiting inside the carriage. In the dim light, Harrison could see that she was dressed in male attire, a dark suit and cravat with a wide-brimmed fedora pulled down to shade her features.

'Good evening, Harrison. I trust you are fully prepared for tonight's venture.'

'Yes,' he said, holding up a small bag of tools provided by Moran to Harrison's specification.

'Good.' A ghost of a smile haunted her features briefly but faded in an instant. Rapping the roof of the carriage with her walking cane as a signal for Bassick to set forth, she sat back and sighed gently. The carriage lurched forwards into the night.

For the most part they travelled in silence. This time the route was not as circuitous as on previous occasions, although the shutters were closed so that Harrison could not see out. As they neared their destination, Cordelia Moriarty checked her pocket watch. 'We have made good time,' she said. 'Bassick will drop us a few streets away from the bank.'

Harrison was not a man to give way to nerves. He was generally able to focus his mind precisely on the matter in hand and sublimate any extraneous emotions that threatened to divert him from his task. However, usually this was because he was well aware of the outcome of his actions. He was able to weigh up the possibilities and probabilities of the situation and prepare himself for a selection of eventualities. Not so in this case. A small grey cloud of uncertainty hovered on the horizon. A challenge it undoubtedly was, but he was determined to be equal to it.

The carriage slewed to a halt. 'We're here, madam,' came Bassick's muffled voice.

Harrison stepped out into the empty street followed by Cordelia Moriarty. It was quite dark now and the area was ill-lit, with few gas lamps to illuminate the night. 'Follow me,' she said in hushed tones and set off at a brisk pace. They crossed a few streets before turning down a narrow alley and reaching the rear of the bank. Passing through the iron gates, Cordelia Moriarty led Harrison to the rear door. This was also unlocked. Entering the gloomy vestibule, she whistled, the shrill notes echoing in the building. It was answered by another whistle and shortly there appeared an indistinct figure carrying an oil lamp. Harrison assumed this was the night watchman in the pay of the Organisation.

'Evenin' ma'am,' he said in rasping voice.

'Wilkins?'

'That's me, ma'am.'

'Is all as it should be?'

Wilkins gave a throaty laugh. 'All is ship shape and Bristol fashion.'

'Then lead us to the safe.'

They passed down the corridor and entered a cavernous chamber, in the centre of which was the large safe. It dominated the room.

'Quite a beast to contain such a small item,' observed Cordelia Moriarty. She turned to Harrison. 'There is your challenge.'

He nodded and knelt beside it, examining the dial, the centre of the door and the two handles either side of it. 'Bring the lamp nearer,' he said as he placed his bag of tools on the floor. Wilkins did as he was asked, and Harrison withdrew a stethoscope from the bag. Now the performance was about to begin. Securing the earpieces in position, he placed the bell head section close to the dial and began to move it infinitesimally slowly. This performance went on for some five minutes in absolute silence. Eventually Harrison turned to Cordelia Moriarty with a sigh. 'They are very cunning people, I'll say that for them.'

'Not too cunning for you, I hope,' came the sour reply.

Harrison did not respond but turned his attention back to his task. His preliminary investigations had satisfied him that Mycroft had arranged for the locking mechanism to be simplified to allow him to open the safe with comparative ease, but he knew he had to put on a show in order to be convincing. He removed a small chisel and hammer from his bag and tapped the dial delicately before placing the tools on the ground. Clamping the stethoscope to the door of the safe, he began to turn the dial slowly.

Wilkins the night watchman stood in the shadows like a statue in silence, holding the oil lamp close to the safe to provide sufficient illumination for Harrison's endeavours.

'Drag that stool over and put the lamp on it,' he told Wilkins. He was not comfortable with the night watchman's close surveillance. The old fellow did as he was instructed.

After another five minutes of slowly rotating the dial, Harrison gave a satisfying murmur. Leaning back, he turned one of the brass handles in a ninety-degree arc.

'Halfway there,' he said.

Cordelia Moriarty gave a nod of approval but her features remained neutral.

Chapter Thirty-seven

In a dank cell in Scotland Yard, Colonel Sebastian Moran lit up the last of his cigars from his Moroccan leather case and leaned back on the thin sacking that served as a bed. With an indulgent sigh, he exhaled the blue smoke towards the cracked and sagging ceiling. He knew that, this time, it was the end of the trail. He knew now that the old shikari had participated in his last hunt. The good times had lasted a long while and he was now resigned to his fate: the inevitable long period of imprisonment that was waiting for him – or possibly worse. However, he never expected, even in his wildest dreams, to be apprehended by that man, the one who stuck a pistol in his back and marched him to a waiting Black Maria. There was, he considered, something comic about it. However, it struck him that if he had not decided, on a whim, to replace Wilkins as night watchman, he may well have escaped capture. Foolishly, he had given in to his strong desire to be present when the safe was opened and Moriarty's daughter took possession of the diadem. Such a whim was his downfall and very strangely he found himself quite sanguine about it.

As he lay back and savoured his cigar, he wondered what fate awaited the redoubtable Cordelia Moriarty. Would she escape the clutches of the law or might she soon find herself be in a neighbouring cell? This thought brought a tinge of sadness. He had so wanted her to succeed and indeed, maybe she would. She was a remarkable woman, a fine tribute to her father.

Irish was just nodding off to sleep in a chair, a half empty mug of beer by his side, when his senses were fully aroused by a commotion at the main door of the Dormitory. 'What the…' he cried as he saw the great door begin to splinter and break asunder. Moments later it collapsed, and a body of uniformed policeman crowded through the aperture. So mesmerised was he by this sight that Irish froze momentarily to the spot and was not quick enough to move before a burly constable grabbed him. Thrusting his arms behind his back, the policeman clapped a pair of handcuffs on Irish. 'We've come for you and all your felonious inmates here,' the constable growled. 'We have some comfortable quarters for you all elsewhere.'

Irish grimaced and, turning his head, he saw a blue line haring upstairs, truncheons in hand.

With a further click of the dial, which, despite its tiny sound, was clearly audible in the silent cellar, Harrison leaned back from his labours for a moment before turning the second brass handle and then as he pulled hard on it, the large door of the safe swung open in a slow, almost stately fashion.

Cordelia Moriarty snatched up the oil lamp and advanced at speed. 'Get back,' she said sharply. 'Get out of the way.'

Harrison scrambled aside as she held the lamp aloft, illuminating the contents of the safe. The large grey interior, housing a single shelf, contained one item: a long jewellery case, of slim design and tooled in finely gilded scarlet leather. She reached inside and snatched it up. Replacing the oil lamp on the stool, she opened the box and gasped as she revealed the contents. Inside was the Josephine Necklace. It was a thing of great beauty and it sparkled brightly in the flickering light of the lamp. Cordelia Moriarty lifted it from the box and held it to her breast.

'It is magnificent,' she said softly, her face aglow with pleasure.

'A nice trinket indeed,' observed Harrison.

On hearing his voice, her features darkened and very swiftly she returned the necklace to its case, which she then slipped inside her jacket pocket.

'You have done well, Harrison. Hasn't he, Wilkins?'

It took a few seconds for the night watchman to reply with a simple, throaty, 'Yes, ma'am.'

'A job well done. Now it is time for your reward, as promised.'

She reached inside her trouser pocket, produced a small pistol and aimed it at Harrison's heart.

Chapter Thirty-eight

Harrison had not been expecting this so soon, but he managed to remain calm and self-contained. 'What is this all about?' he said with a hint of amusement in his voice as though he assumed that Cordelia Moriarty's threat was some kind of joke.

'It is the end, I'm afraid. Your usefulness is over. Skilled safecrackers can be found easily. I have what I want and now you are surplus to my needs. I am afraid you know too much about me and my Organisation and so you are a threat to my security. You must see that, Mr Holmes?'

It was one of those rare moments in his life when Sherlock Holmes was struck dumb with shock.

Cordelia Moriarty smiled at his unease. 'It has gradually dawned on me who you were. Who was this brilliant fellow who had emerged out of nowhere, I wondered. A suspicious nature never lies dormant. As you might say: when you have eliminated the impossible whatever remains… However, I have to congratulate you on a brilliant performance. You are a fine actor, Mr Holmes. Too good in a way. However, you have given me the great pleasure of seeing you, the famous detective of Baker Street, commit a robbery for me. For you it is rather an embarrassing end to your otherwise illustrious career. Now the deed is done, I have to be pragmatic in these matters, I'm afraid.' She extended the hand holding the gun when Wilkins, the night watchman, stepped forwards and with a downward thrust of his arm knocked the weapon from her grasp. It clattered to the floor. In an instant, he had stooped down and snatched it up.

'What on earth are you doing?' she cried.

Wilkins gave a little laugh, the rough throatiness now having disappeared. 'I'm saving the life of my good friend, Sherlock Holmes,' he said, throwing off his rather disreputable flat cap.

'Great heavens, is that you really you, Watson?' said Holmes in utter amazement.

'Indeed. Well, of course it is. Where else would I be?'

'Sherlock Holmes!' cried Cordelia Moriarty. 'Why, you devil!' she screamed, running towards him, her arms extended, the hands like claws ready to tear at his face, but he was prepared for her and he grabbed each wrist in a firm hold.

'Take care, lady. Watson here has an easy trigger finger.'

She froze for a moment and slumped back in apparent despair. Holmes released his grasp.

'What does this all mean?' she asked in a strange staccato fashion.

'It means it is all over. Your dream of resurrecting your father's criminal organisation has been reduced to ashes.'

'Because of you, Sherlock Holmes.'

'I suppose so, but in many ways you have only yourself to

blame. Remember you came to me in the beginning, not I to you. You were determined to humiliate and then destroy me. You enticed me into your world. Had you left me alone, I may well have been unable to penetrate your veil of secrecy.'

'I wanted you dead because you killed my father. It was my duty to revenge his death.'

'A revenge from the grave, eh? That was perhaps your greatest mistake. Like your father's. You underestimated me also.'

For a moment it looked as though Cordelia Moriarty was about to renew her attack on Holmes, but the flames of anger quickly died away. Her face and demeanour now registered wretchedness and the gaze of a woman quickly calculating her options and finding them wanting.

Holmes turned to his old friend and patted his arm. 'Once more, I am in your debt, Watson.'

'I was happy to be part of the game,' he said.

Holmes chuckled. 'And a master of disguise.'

'I learned a few tricks from you,' he said, tearing off his monstrous side whiskers.

'Oh,' said Holmes, with a grin, 'now I recognise you. Ah, well, I think it is time we escorted the lady outside. I trust the police wagon is waiting.'

'Indeed. As you instructed. Lestrade is in charge of the matter.'

Holmes turned to Cordelia Moriarty, who had fallen silent, her shoulders slumped as though in resignation. Holmes made a gentle gesture with his hand towards the door. 'Shall we go?' he said softly.

She shrugged. 'It appears I have no option. Whatever you think of me, I am a realist. I know when I am beaten.'

The imposing dark silhouette of a police vehicle was standing in the street, along with another carriage and about six policemen. Amongst them was the lean figure of Inspector Giles Lestrade. On seeing Sherlock Holmes, he smiled broadly and touched his hat in salute. 'Looks like you did it all right, Mr Holmes,' he said cheerfully.

'It would appear so,' replied the detective.

'I assume this is the lady in question.'

'You are on brilliant form tonight, Inspector. Yes, this is Miss Cordelia Moriarty, the daughter of the late lamented Professor James Moriarty.'

Lestrade sniffed. 'Lamented by some, but not me.' Turning to one of the constables he added, 'Right, Booth, get her in the wagon.'

The constable threw open the door and approached her with a set of handcuffs. Holmes was surprised how docile she seemed now. Her arrogance and ferocious demeanour had vanished altogether. She now presented a picture of a broken woman.

As the constable made a gesture to take his prisoner's manacled arm to help her into the cab there was a brief spark of anger in those lustrous eyes. 'I can manage on my own,' she said. The voice was low and firm. Before she disappeared into the van, Cordelia Moriarty turned round and gazed at Holmes. 'Game set and match, eh, Sherlock?' she said before retreating into the darkness.

'Quite a woman, eh, Watson?'

The doctor nodded, 'Formidable and rather frightening.'

'Right Booth,' said Lestrade turning to a red-faced constable, 'you travel in the back with madam and you, Fletcher, can ride up with me up front.'

Holmes leaned forward and touched Lestrade's sleeve. 'Before you take your leave, there is one other fellow you need to apprehend. If you send several your men around to Carlton Street, two blocks away, you will find Milady's carriage and her butler associate, a fellow named Bassick, waiting for her return. He needs to be added to your haul.'

'Right you are, Mr Holmes. I'll see to it.'

'Well, Watson, shall we leave friend Lestrade to it? Would you care for a brief stroll before we hail a late-night cab to take us back to Baker Street; get some fresh cold night air into our lungs?'

Watson smiled. 'That sounds like a good idea.'

The two friends strolled down the street as the police wagon rumbled past them at a stately pace.

Inside, Cordelia Moriarty sat on a wooden bench across from Constable Booth who, against regulations, had lit up a cigarette. 'Do you want one, dearie? Don't mind you having a smoke, a final pleasure before all that's going to happen to you.' His fleshy lips flickered into a smile.

She shook her head. 'No, thank you.' Her words were hardly audible.

Booth sat back, content with his cigarette and failed to observe his prisoner reach her handcuffed hands down towards her feet and slip one hand into the side vent of her right boot. Slowly she withdrew a slim folding knife and secreted it in her palm.

After a few minutes, she then gave a groan and slumped sideways.

'What's the matter?' asked Booth, dismayed that the smooth progress of the journey and his pleasurable smoke was being interrupted.

'I think I'm going to be sick. I have to be near a window when I'm travelling,' she moaned, folding herself up into a foetal position. Booth stubbed his cigarette out with irritation and moved towards her. He was not much concerned about the health of the prisoner but more intrigued by this sudden change in her behaviour and alert to any subterfuge. As he leaned over her, she turned and thrust the knife deep into his stomach. He gave a muffled gasp and staggered backwards, his eyes wide with shock. In an instant Cordelia Moriarty was on her feet and stabbed him again – this time in the neck. Blood gushed forth and he gave a gargling croak as he sank to his knees, his body shaking in the death tremens before it ceased to move altogether.

Very swiftly she retrieved the key ring from Booth's belt and, with nimble manipulation, released herself from the handcuffs that bound her wrists. She allowed herself a brief smile of triumph before making her way to the rear of the wagon. Another key unlocked it, and she slipped the large bolt of the door, which swung open easily, revealing the night and the road beyond. The vehicle was traversing a series of side streets on the way to its destination. She sat down on the floor with her legs dangling over the edge and waited patiently while it reached a junction where the wagon slowed down to a gentler pace. Now was the time. Taking a deep breath, she jumped down into the street. She stumbled forward but managed to retain her equilibrium, and ran swiftly after the wagon, managing to close the door to prevent it from banging. As the vehicle disappeared into the darkness, she reached the pavement and ran in the opposite direction.

Chapter Thirty-nine

ᏇᎧ

From the journal of John H. Watson

It was past midnight when Holmes and I entered our rooms at Baker Street after the dramatic events of the evening at the City and Counties bank.

'I must admit,' said Holmes, shrugging off his disreputable jacket, 'I never expected you to take such an active role in the finale of this exploit but I am so glad you did, and applaud you for it. You carried off the role magnificently. I had no idea it was you beneath that tattered cap and those monstrous side-whiskers.'

These words of praise warmed my heart. 'Well, to be honest, Holmes, I felt so impotent and frustrated regarding this case, just having to contribute occasionally to Mycroft's plans and wait around to hear news of you, not being able to support your investigations in any practical way, that in the end I became determined to involve myself in a physical fashion. It struck me that in replacing the night watchman, I was providing extra help and support should you need it. Neither Mycroft nor Lestrade were keen on the plan initially, but I managed to talk them round.'

'I'm so glad you did. And not only did you save my life but you also succeeded in securing the arrest of Colonel Moran.'

I gave a brief chuckle. 'That was remarkable. I was expecting the night watchman to turn up at the rear door of the bank, but lo and behold, it was Moran. I was as surprised as he was when I placed my revolver to his head.'

'An excellent night's work, Watson. Now before we indulge in a celebratory nightcap, I must wash and change. I have lived as Harrison for too long and I am very keen to return to my own clothes and my own features. I know that I will have to wait a while for my hair to grow but I am determined that this dreadful moustache and beard will very soon become a horrid memory. I want to return to being Sherlock Holmes.'

With these words, he disappeared into his bedroom. Within half an hour we were sitting opposite each other by the fireside, a glass of brandy in our hands. It was good to see him restored to his almost familiar self. He lay back casually, wrapped in his mouse-coloured dressing-gown, his gaunt features smooth and no longer marred by the hairy upper lip and livid scar. This had been a self-administered surface cut along the prominent plane of his cheekbone, cunningly enhanced with make-up and still faintly visible. However, I was sure that in a few months it would disappear altogether.

'I must say this has been one of the most remarkable cases of my career; complex and challenging,' he said. 'And it brought me into contact with one of the most cunning and dangerous female adversaries I have ever encountered, the spawn of the Napoleon of Crime himself.'

At the very reference to Moriarty, I shuddered. 'She was a she-devil in human form.'

Holmes smiled indulgently. 'Ah, there's the writer in you. But she was a wicked woman indeed. What a pity that someone with intelligence, fortitude and personal magnetism should follow the left-hand path.'

'What is her history? How is it that we knew nothing of her?'

Holmes was just about to respond to my query where there a came a noise as of thunder from down below. Someone was hammering on our front door. Without a word, we both raced downstairs and threw open the door. Inspector Lestrade almost fell into our arms. I could tell immediately that he was in a terrible state: his face was bathed in sweat; his tie was askew and his eyes were rolling wildly as though he was caught in some kind of delirious trance.

'Catastrophe,' he croaked, shaking his head wildly. 'It is terrible.'

'Let us get him upstairs and give him some brandy,' said Holmes grabbing Lestrade by the arm and leading him towards the stairs.

Once ensconced in an armchair with a glass of brandy in his hand, our friend's mania began to diminish.

'In simple terms, what is the dilemma that has reduced you to this state of distress?' asked Holmes, lighting up his clay pipe.

Lestrade shook his head wildly from side to side. 'She's gone, Mr Holmes. Escaped.'

Neither Holmes nor I had any need to enquire to whom this 'she' was.

'What the devil!' cried Holmes, his features suffused with fury. 'How could this have happened? Explain yourself.'

'She must have had a concealed weapon. She attacked the constable in the back of the wagon. Stabbed him to death and escaped. Leapt out, no doubt, somewhere *en route*. We only found out when we got to the Yard. The wagon was empty apart from the bloody corpse of my constable. The bird had flown.'

Holmes slapped his forehead in frustrated anger. 'Of all the incompetent...' He stopped short, knowing that Lestrade already felt bad enough, and that he should have specified a higher level of security when communicating his plans at the Diogenes Club. Cordelia Moriarty had taken advantage of the situation.

Lestrade leant forward in his chair and ran his bony fingers across his brow. 'What do we do now, Mr Holmes?' he asked, his voice strained with emotion. I must admit that I felt sorry for the fellow.

Holmes did not reply to Lestrade's agonised request, but paced up and down on the hearth rug, puffing away furiously at his pipe, his brow contracted in thought. Then suddenly he stopped as though frozen to the spot, his eyes flashing brightly.

'That's it,' he cried. 'Watson, make a long arm and retrieve the Bradshaw from the shelf.'

I did so.

'Good, now check the time of the boat train to the continent in the morning. If memory serves me, there is one leaving Victoria at 7.30 a.m.'

I riffled through the pages. Holmes was correct. The first continental express was due to depart at that hour.

'What's all this about?' asked Lestrade.

'Cordelia Moriarty has spent most of her life in France. Now that she is on the run, a fugitive, it is logical that she will attempt to return to the continent where she can easily disappear, lose herself somewhere away from the tentacles of British justice. No doubt she has several boltholes there. She certainly will not want to find refuge in this country with the whole of our police force searching for her. We must catch her before she leaves these shores. The quickest way for her to get to France is by the boat train. No doubt the lady will attempt to catch the earliest one – at seven thirty this morning.' He consulted his watch. 'That is in five hours' time.'

'Well, if what you say is true, Mr Holmes, I'll have a body of men at the station ready to nab her.'

'No, no. They would easily frighten her away. We do not want that. This must be handled more subtly. Besides, she will no doubt be in some disguise and not that easy to detect. I ask you to leave the matter to me.'

Lestrade hesitated a moment and then nodded decisively. 'Very well. I have put my trust in you in the past and you have never let me down. And I must say, your actions in this current business have been exemplary.'

Holmes gave a deferential smile. 'You are very kind, friend Lestrade. Indeed, we have the gang, the tentacles; it is just the head of the monster we now need to secure, and I feel certain that this will be achieved in the morning. If you'll give leave...'

'Very well,' Lestrade said, both his voice and demeanour weary.

'Then it is settled,' replied Holmes. 'Now I suggest you get yourself home to bed and secure a good night's rest. I am sure that I will have news for you before noon.'

Lestrade acquiesced to Holmes' suggestion without further persuasion and shambled from the room.

'What do you intend to do tomorrow?' I asked.

Holmes gave me a tight grin. 'More of that later. We have one more assignment tonight before our heads hit the pillow.'

I raised my eyebrows in surprise. 'What on earth is that?'

'A little chat with our old friend Colonel Sebastian Moran.'

In our cab ride to Scotland Yard, Holmes emphasised that we must in no way let Moran know that Cordelia had escaped. 'That will only create sparks of hope in his tired brain. I want him at his most malleable.'

'I fully understand,' said I, while wondering what Holmes was intending to do.

Half an hour later we entered the cell at Scotland Yard where Moran was ensconced. He was asleep but we had no difficulty in rousing him. He showed little surprise at our presence.

'Mr Holmes and his lap dog Watson. To what do I owe this honour?'

Holmes withdrew a brandy flask from his coat. 'I bring you a little comfort. Something to warm the blood. I know how bleak and chilly these cells can be.' He handed the flask to Moran, who with a little hesitation took it from him.

'It's not poisoned, is it?'

Holmes chuckled. 'You know me well enough to be sure that I would not do such a thing. I am a law-abiding citizen.'

With a sudden movement Moran removed the top of the flask and took a big gulp. 'My, it is brandy and good brandy. A kind gesture, Mr Holmes, but I suspect you will require something in return.'

My friend nodded. 'Astute as ever, Colonel.'

'As you can see from my... somewhat reduced circumstances I have little to offer.'

'I want information.'

'I thought you might.'

'As you know, we have Cordelia Moriarty in custody, but she is refusing to talk. A mistake on her part. To reveal any extenuating circumstances concerned with her criminal activities would no doubt help her case when it comes to trial.'

'You think so?' There was a sneering tone to Moran's response.

'Believe me, I do. As for myself, I wish to complete the picture that this wild scenario has created. There are shadowy areas where things are not clear. I could make inspired, intelligent assumptions...'

'Deductions, eh. Eliminating the impossible to reach out for the improbable.'

'If you like. But in this instance the probable is not sufficient. I want certainty. The truth.'

'What makes you so sure that I possess such knowledge, that I know the truth, or, indeed, that I would be willing to share it?'

'You have a long history with James Moriarty, and you have worked closely with his daughter.'

Moran took another drink of brandy. 'Yes, you are right.' He sighed. 'I miss the old fellow very much. I believe I knew him as well as anyone could, but it was only at the very end that I learned about his daughter.'

'Tell me said Sherlock Holmes softly. 'Tell me for her sake. No harm can come to you by revealing all now.'

Moran's eyes moistened and took on a faraway look. They seemed to peer in the darkness beyond Holmes.

When he spoke, it was as though he was talking to himself rather than in response to Holmes' entreaty. 'Why not? As you intimate, I have nothing further to lose.'

As we sat in that cold gloomy cell both my friend and I were mesmerised by Colonel Moran's narrative. As he talked, I made notes, as I always did in such circumstances. I report it here in a dramatised form in full, relying on these notes and my memory, which retains a most vivid impression of Moran's account.

Chapter Forty

ℰ

Moran's Story

It was when we landed in France on the first stage of our trek in pursuit of Sherlock Holmes – a trek that eventually led to Switzerland and the Reichenbach Falls – that I learned of Professor Moriarty's daughter. It was after dinner one evening as we savoured brandy and cigars that the Professor raised the subject, much to my great surprise.

'When we have put paid to Mr Holmes and returned to England, we shall have the major task of restoring the Organisation,' he said. 'However, in this endeavour, I shall have the assistance of my daughter.'

At this statement, I almost dropped my brandy glass. 'Your daughter,' I cried. 'I… I had no idea you had a daughter.'

Moriarty gave a wan smile. 'I had almost forgotten myself. Until a few days ago she was a distant fragmented memory – a lost ghost from my past. But now she will be very much an active part of my future and the future of the Organisation.'

'But the Organisation has been routed, surely. Holmes' documents sent to Scotland Yard ensured that.'

'So he thought. So I thought, but thanks to the cunning actions of my clever daughter Cordelia, and my contacts at the Yard, she has managed to reduce the damage. It is true that many minor villains have been rounded up, but a small number of our senior officers remain safe and in readiness for my eventual return. With effort and my daughter's help it will not take me long to build up our strength again.'

'Why that is wonderful. Miraculous!'

Moriarty gave a dry chuckle. 'It does indeed seem to have elements of the miraculous about it, does it not? But in truth it is the result of clever chicanery, mainly due to the machinations carried out by Cordelia in my absence.'

'She is a woman I would very much like to meet.'

'Oh, you shall in good time.'

'Why have you not mentioned her before? What is her history?'

The Professor paused for a moment, his eyes flickering with uncertainty. He was obviously deciding whether he should reveal all or retain the secret of this mysterious child. In the end, he gave a decisive nod. 'I will tell you everything, but in complete confidence. I trust no one with this information except you. Is that clear?'

I nodded.

'It may assist you in your dealings with her in the future but it must remain a secret between you and I.' He paused for a moment before continuing. 'I must say that it will do me good to recount this part of my life that I have kept hidden, and indeed, suppressed for so many years.' He took a sip of brandy before continuing.

'The girl was the result of a foolish affair when I was at university. Her mother died in childbirth. I arranged for her care initially in a private nursery, and then with a governess, but as my criminal activities began to grow, I saw the child as an encumbrance. In simple terms, I wanted to be rid of her. She could easily become a bargaining tool with some enemy of mine. I was conscious of the precarious nature of the situation. So, I arranged for her to move to France and be educated there. It was all done swiftly and easily. I provided funds for her upkeep and initially we corresponded, but as she grew older, I stopped responding to her letters, which were tinged with sentimentality and the desire to come back to England and see me. I knew that must not happen.

'I never saw the girl as an adult, although I received a few photographs of her as she grew to be a young woman, but in later years the correspondence faded away. Over time, I thought less and less of her, content to know she was safe in France and making her own way in the world. I really neither knew nor cared what she did after her education ceased. She was no longer part of my life or my responsibility. I had as Shakespeare put it, wiped her from my "trivial fond records". I continued to send a sum of money every month to a bank in Paris and that was all the contact I desired. The money eased what very little conscience I had in abandoning the girl.' Moriarty stubbed out his cigar and gave me a wry grin. 'And then, after many years, she returned.'

'Returned?'

'Yes, a few nights ago. I was alone in my study. It was late and I had just poured a glass of sherry and sat for a while in quiet contemplation. After a time, I raised my glass as though in a toast. "Goodbye, Mr Sherlock Holmes. It has been a duel between us, but all duels end in one fatality – and I'm afraid it is to be yours."

'As I drained my glass, the door of my chamber opened, and a silhouetted figure appeared in the aperture. In an instant, I reached for my revolver on the shelf below my desk.

'"Now, now, Father, don't be so dramatic," came a voice from the gloom. "Surely you're not going to shoot your only daughter?"'

'The figure stepped forward into the faint amber glow emanating from the candle, which illuminated pale and striking features. I stared in disbelief at the young woman who stood before me. So disconcerted was I by this vision that I must admit I was temporarily struck dumb.'

'"Is it you? Is it really you?" I asked, eventually finding my voice. She nodded gently and gave me a cool smile.

'I shook my head in consternation. "What on earth are you doing here?"

'"I've come to help you, of course. It is time, Father. Time for me to take my rightful place at your side. You have kept me away far too long."

'You can perhaps understand the wild range of emotions that swept through me on hearing these words,' Moriarty told me.

'Indeed,' I said, 'but surely the overriding one was of excitement.'

'Yes, I suppose it was.'

'You were sure it was your daughter?'

'Yes, I recognised her features from the earlier photographs and she wore the ruby ring which I had sent her many years ago. And besides, a father knows his own. There she was, standing before me, a tall striking young woman with that same mark of determination that I recognised in my own character. She was almost beautiful but something indefinable about her pale lean face robbed her of that distinction. But there was a ferocity and fire in those eyes that marked her out as a Moriarty – a creature of my blood.

'Cordelia quickly made it clear that she had returned for good and with a purpose. She was aware that this was a very vulnerable time in my criminal career. What she suggested, insisted even, made sense. She was aware of the dark threat that Sherlock Holmes posed not only to my own security but to the survival of the Organisation. She gave me a brief resume of her own criminal activities in France under the name of Madame Defarge, which I must say impressed me greatly. I was aware of Le Carnage and it gave me a certain pride. I was taken by her forceful and persuasive plan. It made me smile. My God, I thought, there is no doubt she is my child. She had returned to England to join me, to help restore the Organisation and be a moving force within it. That night I welcomed back my daughter and sealed our new association with a warm embrace.' There was a catch in the Professor's voice as he uttered this last statement.

A month after it was reported in the press that Sherlock Holmes and Professor James Moriarty had perished at the Reichenbach Falls in Switzerland, a meeting was held in the conference room of Pelham House, the secret headquarters of the Organisation. At the head of the table sat the imposing figure of Cordelia Moriarty, still dressed in mourning. I sat on her right hand and on her left was Sir Justin Butterworth, whom the Professor had seduced into handling all the Organisation's financial business. The others assembled, six in all, were those high-ranking officials of the gang who had managed to escape the cull orchestrated by Sherlock Holmes, most of whom were puzzled at being summoned to this meeting by an unknown woman.

I rose and addressed the meeting. 'Welcome, gentlemen. It is good to see you here once more. It seemed that at one point it was not going to be possible thanks to the interference of that damned

Sherlock Holmes – the Devil take his soul.'

There were mumblings of agreement with this sentiment around the table.

'Thanks to the perspicacious forward thinking of the Professor and the efficient cunning of this lady on my right, the damage to our Organisation was limited – hence your presence here today.'

'Who is the lady?' asked one.

'She is someone who had the full trust of the Professor and in many ways was the saviour of the Organisation. But I will let her introduce herself and explain.' I turned and nodded to Miss Moriarty. She returned the gesture and rose to address the group. A hushed silence fell on the room.

'Gentlemen, I welcome you,' she said in a firm authoritative voice. 'You do not know me, but I am Cordelia Moriarty. Your master, the Professor, is my father.'

At this statement there were gasps and murmurs of surprise around the table. She waited until the exclamations had faded into silence.

'Before my father set off to the continent in pursuit of Sherlock Holmes – a search he feared might very well bring about his own demise as well as that of the accursed detective – he set down in writing a document, held by Sir Justin, which states that should he meet such an untimely end, whatever remained of his Organisation and its fortune should fall into my hands.'

There were further murmurs but the shocked men were still coming to terms with the possibility that their leader had an unknown daughter and as yet no one had the courage or temerity to question Cordelia Moriarty's statement.

'I have the document here, gentlemen, if any of you are in doubt,' said Sir Justin, holding up the sheet of vellum, adding, 'I can confirm that the Professor allocated all his finances and the control of the Organisation to his daughter, who stands here before us.'

'That is why I have summoned you all here today,' said Cordelia, leaning forward over the table. 'You were all trusted and respected members of my father's enterprise and I wish you to retain your roles under my leadership. Now we are a depleted force. The Organisation is a mere shadow of its former self but it is my intention to revive it, to infuse it with a new strength. I do not propose just to return it to its former glory within the criminal underworld, but to make it even greater. Not only will it be a financial benefit for all, but it will be a fitting tribute to my father, the great Professor James Moriarty. Are you with me?'

'But you're a woman…' said one voice from the gloom.

She silenced him with a swift glare, the ferocity in her eyes matching that of the much lamented and much feared Professor.

'Yes, a strong woman. And a Moriarty. I can assure you I am no novice when it comes to organising criminal machinations. For some years I was known as Madame Defarge, the moving force behind *Le Carnage* in Paris.'

At this statement there was a quiet gasp of recognition around the table.

'However, I also bring you good news. My father is alive.'

Someone gave a derisive sarcastic laugh. Cordelia fixed him with another icy stare and he shrank back into the shadows.

'I repeat, my father is still alive and recuperating in France. He is of course very weak and his body is severely damaged but in time and with medical assistance it is hoped that he may return to take his rightful place as the leader of the Organisation. In the meantime, he has handed that role to me…'

'Well, it is good news that the old boy is still in the land of the living,' said one, a statement that prompted a round of 'Hear, hear.'

At this juncture, I took this opportunity to rise to my feet again and address the meeting. 'Let me say, gentlemen, that I have full confidence in Miss Moriarty to carry on where her father has been forced to leave off. Be in no doubt she has my full support and allegiance.'

'That's good enough for me,' said one.

'And me,' cried another.

These voices were joined by echoes around the table.

Cordelia held up her hand to silence them. 'I thank you, gentlemen. I assure you that I will not let you down. In the coming months and years this Organisation will grow in numbers and strength and be a tribute to the man who is dubbed "The Napoleon of Crime", my father James Moriarty.'

'What a fancy cock and bull story,' cried one burly fellow, Arthur Dodd, a controller of the gangs in the docklands. 'We all know the Prof is a gonner. A dead 'un. No way could he have survived that drop into that bloody Swiss waterfall. This is all a pack of lies. I don't know what it's all about but I bet it's some cunning plot concocted by Moran and this bit of tail here. Hah, saying she's Moriarty's daughter! Load of baloney! We all know the old chap never had kids. It's a great big trick and I'm not falling for it. You can count me out.'

With a violent gesture, he threw back his chair and headed for the door.

Cordelia took a step towards him. 'Are you sure you are doing the right thing by leaving?'

'I bloody well am,' snarled Dodd.

Without hesitation, Cordelia produced a pistol from her reticule and fired it directly at Dodd. He managed to utter the word, 'No,' before falling dead at Cordelia's feet.

With a cold smile she turned to the others. 'Is there anyone else who doubts my word?' she asked gently.

Sometime later, Cordelia sat quietly with me, each of us drinking a glass of wine.

'That went very well,' she said.

'Your little demonstration concerning the essentials of loyalty was most effective,' I agreed. 'In truth, those men are mere puppets – skilled puppets in their dark crafts – but in need of a puppet master. A clever person who can pull their strings and control their actions with expertise.'

'An interesting analogy. And no doubt you see me as this puppet master – or should that be mistress? I thank you.'

'I must say I wasn't expecting you to claim that the Professor was still alive. That was a surprise to me.'

'I thought it was an added incentive to encourage allegiance. They may not like taking orders from a young woman, but if they believe this to be a temporary measure before the Professor returns, I am sure they will toe the line. And they will soon come to realise that, despite their prejudices and appearances, I will fit perfectly into my father's shoes.'

'I am sure you will. I see it in your eyes.'

'And may I say, Colonel, I am very happy to have your full support. You are the main link with my father and it is a boon and a privilege to have you by my side.'

'I am delighted to be in this position and I assure you it is my life's ambition to aid you in the resurrection of your father's network and in the destruction of the man who brought about his death – that devil Holmes. Somewhere in this world he roams free when he should be at the bottom of the Reichenbach Falls instead of the Professor. But one day he will return to London, I am sure of it. And when he does, I will snuff out his life as easily as one does a candle.'

'I pray for that day also. Such a revenge would help to ease my soul. But I am determined that it will be me who ends his life – his demise is my legacy. Let us drink to that happy day.'

We both raised our glasses and drank a silent toast of affirmation. As it turned out it was a futile dream.

Chapter Forty-one

From the journal of John H. Watson

Holmes and I were both silent on the journey back to Baker Street, as we each digested the details of the sensational account that Colonel Sebastian Moran had provided regarding Moriarty and his daughter. It had been a remarkable revelation and I could see from Holmes' features that he was pleased to have learned the full story and, as he revealed to me later, to have had a number of his own deductions confirmed.

However, as we entered our sitting room at a very late hour, my mind turned to the morning, wondering how Holmes intended to apprehend Cordelia Moriarty before she escaped to the continent.

'What is your plan for the morning?' I asked Holmes.

'Ah, a little *coup de theatre* on my part. A wonderful moment of symmetry and irony.' He chuckled and rubbed his hands together enthusiastically, his eyes alive with excitement.

'What mischief are you planning?'

'If we are to search the train for milady Moriarty, it must be done with stealth. I cannot scrutinise the passengers as myself, as she would easily recognise me and slip through our grasp again. Therefore, I will go in disguise. And what a disguise.'

I raised my brow as a prompt for him to elucidate further.

'You will remember when we travelled to continent in what turned out to be a failed attempt to escape the clutches of Moriarty.'

'Indeed, I do.'

'You met me on the train...'

'My goodness,' I cried suddenly aware at what Holmes was suggesting. 'You were dressed as an Italian priest – an aged Italian priest. You were very convincing.'

'*Grazie mille.* Indeed, a priest, the epitome of an innocent fellow who means no harm to anyone.'

'And where do I fit into this scenario?' I asked somewhat petulantly.

'In the shadows waiting on the platform, I am afraid, but it is an important role for, if the lady attempts to make a bolt for it, it may very well be left to you to stop her. Therefore, it would be wise to bring along your revolver.'

With a reluctant nod, I resigned myself once more to a subservient role.

Holmes stretched and yawned. 'It has been a long weary day for both of us, Watson, but it's not over yet. Take a brief nap if you must while I prepare for the morning's trials and adopt my disguise. We have little time before our next adventure. We need to be ready to leave for Victoria Station at six o'clock in preparation to write the final chapter of this dark and challenging affair.'

Chapter Forty-Two

From the journal of John H. Watson

When we set off at six for Victoria Station, I had no notion that the events of the morning would take such a surprising and tragic turn. Although my involvement in what occurred was small, Holmes was later to recount in detail the drama that took place. He emerged from his dressing room disguised, as he had promised, as an ancient Italian priest and looked most convincing in the role with the long cassock and grey wig topped by a wide brimmed saturno hat. It was the exact outfit he had worn on that fateful day some three years ago when we left London with the Professor on our heels. Holmes carried with him a capacious valise. I could see from the twinkle in his eyes that he was pleased to don the disguise once more for his encounter with Moriarty's daughter. As he had intimated, there was a kind of poetic symmetry to the occasion, but this time he was the hound and a Moriarty was the prey.

Holmes sketched out his plan of action as we travelled to the railway station.

'It is imperative that we split up before we reach the platform for the continental express. You must stay in the shadows, keeping out of sight as much as possible. Miss Moriarty has met you, and your skills in disguise, though surprisingly effective, are not as polished as my own. Despite my new persona, if she saw me with you, the game would be over. I am certain that she will also have altered her own appearance in some way. Remember her performance as Elizabeth Courtney? We both must scrutinise the passengers very carefully. If you spot her before I do, you must come and inform me immediately, but do not approach her unless absolutely necessary. She would not think twice about killing you. Remember that poor constable.'

'I will do as you ask,' I replied gravely.

We hailed two cabs outside our lodgings and, travelling separately from this point onwards we each purchased tickets on arrival at Victoria and made our way to platform seven from where the continental express was due to depart. It was a quarter to seven and the train was already in situ but the guard informed me that the doors would not be opened until a quarter past the hour.

As arranged, I had positioned myself close to the barrier behind a pillar while Holmes strolled casually along the platform. There were already a few passengers milling around waiting for the doors to be released and as the time passed there came a steady stream of more travellers making their way through the ticket barrier. I gazed hard at each face, but I could see no one whom I thought resembled Cordelia Moriarty in any way. I glanced down the platform to see if Holmes was having better luck. From his glum expression it appeared not.

It reached quarter past seven and as the doors were opened there was a general rush to board the train. To my surprise, I saw that Holmes was attempting to do so also and had requested the assistance of a porter to help him enter the compartment and to carry his bag. It was only later that I learned what was really happening.

Chapter Forty-three

❧

Sherlock Holmes tapped the porter on the shoulder. '*Mi scusi, signore*, would you please assist me to board? My old bones are failing me and I have such a heavy bag also,' he croaked.

The attendant simply nodded and, placing his arm under that of the priest, assisted him to mount the step and make his way into the compartment.

'*Grazie, signore.* Now if you would be so kind, could you bring in my bag and place it on the rack for me.'

Without a word, the attendant clambered into the compartment and hoisted the valise on to the luggage rack. As he did so, Holmes moved to the door and pulled it shut. The porter turned swiftly at the noise and saw the old priest standing with his back to the door with a pistol in in hand. He was smiling.

'This is a very theatrical moment, is it not?' he said, the croaky voice and Italian accent having disappeared. 'Old enemies meeting like this, each pretending to be someone else: me an aged Italian cleric... and you a lowly railway attendant. A very convincing one, Miss Moriarty, apart from one flaw in your makeup.'

'Oh?' she said quietly, with no emotion, her features remaining still.

Holmes held up his hand and wiggled his finger. 'The ring. The ruby ring on your right hand. You really should have taken it off, you know. One does not see a young man in a porter's uniform wearing a ruby ring of such quality.'

'It was a present from my father. I wear it always.'

Holmes smiled. 'Ah, so no doubt you couldn't bear to be parted from your father's keepsake and wore it for sentimental reasons. A touching gesture, I admit. It reveals that there is some softness in that cold heart of yours. But my dear Miss Moriarty...' He wiggled his finger again. 'It was a mistake.'

She gave a gentle shrug and removed her cap, allowing her hair to fall about her face. 'So, what do you intend to do now?'

'Well, it seems that I have the upper hand, does it not? I believe this pistol is my ace. It is time for me to escort you to Scotland Yard where you can begin paying for your misdemeanours, including the murder of a young constable.'

For the first time Cordelia Moriarty showed some emotion. She smiled. 'Needs must, Mr Holmes. The fellow was in my way – as you are now. You do not think I will come with you quietly or easily. I do not believe that you will shoot me. You have a humane streak running through you and that is a palpable weakness. However, I assure you that the only way you will win this battle is by putting a bullet through my heart. You hope to place me in the dock; I tell you that I will never stand in the dock.'

Holmes felt a chill at these words. They were the very ones used by her father when he came to Baker Street to threaten him all those years ago. Whether she was aware of this or by some freak of coincidence she had mouthed the Professor's utterances, he did not know.

'I spent many years of exile in France – imposed on me by Father because he did not want me involved in his life and his activities. It was an act of love and protection. That was how I interpreted it. I returned, determined to reconnect with him and support him in running his Organisation. To my delight he welcomed me with open arms and I saw a bright future working with him, reaffirming the bonds between us as father and daughter. And then you… you took him away from me.' There was a catch in her voice as she uttered this last sentence.

'One of my strongest desires when I took over my father's Organisation was to destroy you – his murderer,' she continued. 'It was to be a kind of revenge from the grave but unfortunately you have slipped through my net, and now I have to accept the inevitable that you will survive – for the moment at least.'

'I had not expected idle threats, Miss Moriarty. You must realise that the game is up. There is no future for you apart from the steps to the gallows.'

Cordelia Moriarty shook her head vigorously. 'I shall not hang. If I am to die, I will choose my own end.' She took a step towards Holmes, producing a knife from her jacket pocket. 'You can shoot me as I stab you, you devil. We will die together.' With a savage cry of fury, she lunged forward at Holmes with the knife.

Just at that moment the carriage jolted violently and juddered as the train began to leave the station. Holmes was thrown sideways by the sudden jerking movement and Cordelia Moriarty also lost her balance. She fell to the floor, the knife slipping from her grasp. In an instant, Holmes stooped down and retrieved it.

'No more melodramatics please, Miss Moriarty,' he said, helping her to her feet.

She pulled herself away from him and to Holmes' surprise, she was laughing.

'When it comes down to it, Mr Holmes, for all your intellectual brilliance, you have to rely on male brute force and a gun to succeed.'

'Not unlike the methods used by your father at our last meeting. One must fight evil with all the means at one's command. Our battle is now over. There is nothing further you can do to escape the consequences of your criminal career. We shall depart this train at the next station, where I will deliver you into the hands of the police authorities.'

'That is not an agreeable arrangement to me,' she said moving to the far side of the compartment. They stared at each other in silence for several minutes as the train gathered pace.

Finally, with a minute flicker of her eyes towards the window, she smiled and said, 'I prefer to be in charge of my own destiny.'

She turned abruptly and flung open the carriage door. A blast of cold air swept into the compartment as the train sped along, released from the confines of the city.

'Goodbye, Mr Holmes,' she cried as she jumped from the carriage. As she disappeared from sight, Holmes could hear her screams blending with the noise of the engine. He ran to the doorway and gazed out but a curve in the track had robbed him of the chance of seeing anything of her. Cordelia Moriarty's body was no doubt lying at the side of the track some distance beyond his vision. Slowly he closed the door and sat down, somewhat taken aback by events. He had never expected that Cordelia Moriarty would take her own life. There was little chance of survival after jumping from a train moving at speed. She had ended her life as she had lived it, with a self-possessed determination to take independent control of her own actions whatever the cost. She was an evil woman, but Holmes had to admit that she was also a remarkable one.

Chapter Forty-four

From the journal of John H. Watson

A week after the demise of Cordelia Moriarty, Holmes and I found ourselves taking a late afternoon walk in Kensington Gardens. Although my friend had initially related the events that took place in the railway carriage of the continental express to both Lestrade and myself, he had been reluctant to discuss them further. I knew Holmes well enough not to question him in an attempt to gain more insight into the case and his feelings. For some days he had kept his own counsel and so I was a little surprised when he suggested that we take a stroll in the gardens. As we did so, he began to talk about the case. It was as though he had felt that the moment had come when he could unburden himself.

It was one of those September afternoons when it seemed that summer would never end and yet one could smell the early autumn chill lay hidden beneath the heat. The foliage was already showing signs of turning to the golds and browns of its late season plumage. I could sense that Holmes was in a melancholy mood as we strolled by the lake.

'It has been a remarkable summer,' he mused. 'I never thought in my wildest dreams that I would find myself locking horns, as it were, with a Moriarty once more.'

'And a female one.'

Holmes gave a gentle grin. 'Indeed. It seems such a pity that such an intelligent and capable woman should be tainted with the evil traits of her father.'

'I remember you once saying something about art in the blood. I suppose it is a case that one cannot avoid one's destiny.'

'Nicely put, you old literary gent. But she was a remarkable woman – one of my greatest foes. Reading through various secret papers and the Professor's private journals taken from Pelham House, along with certain communications I have received from Mycroft provided by his contacts in the Sûreté, I have been able to construct a general biography of Cordelia Moriarty.'

'I should be most interested in hearing about her early years,' I said eagerly, 'before what Moran was able to tell us.'

'Well, to start at the beginning we must return to the year 1853. It was at this time that James Moriarty was in his last year at university and was involved in a relationship with a young woman, the daughter of his tutor. When the girl became pregnant, Moriarty saw his career as a brilliant mathematician crumbling before his eyes. The prospect of being saddled with a woman and a child was abhorrent to his calculating mind and cold heart. With the help of his lover's spinster aunt, she agreed to escape to France on the pretext of attending an academy there. Sadly, she died in childbirth and the baby was brought up by the aunt in Paris until she died, when the girl was about twelve. It seems that at this point young Cordelia took charge of her own destiny and continued her studies. To Moriarty's credit he did at least continue to provide financial support for his daughter, although there was little actual contact between the two and none from the Professor after the aunt's demise. She was left independently secure after her death. It was as though the Professor had eradicated her from his mind as an inconvenience.

'After the death of his lover, it is quite clear that Moriarty became determined that he should never allow such distractions to interfere with his life again. Effectively, he erased from his personality what few softer passions there may have been as a young man, growing colder, pathologically dark, and more skilled in the art of deceit. Very soon his mind turned towards the criminal path. As you know over the intervening years, Moriarty grew in stature as a felonious mastermind...'

'The Napoleon of crime.'

'Indeed. In the meantime, Cordelia having inherited her father's criminal genes, began to follow in his footsteps and by her early twenties, she was operating a small gang in Paris known as Le Carnage. As you know, she ran the operation using the soubriquet Madame Defarge. After a time she wanted to spread her wings a little wider, and when she learned on the grapevine that I was posing a threat to her father's Organisation, she came to England to present the Professor with a plan to assist him. With his extensive web of underworld contacts he would have knowledge of the Defarge gang but I doubt if he knew that it was operated by his daughter. At this pivotal moment in his criminal career, Moriarty welcomed her with open arms and into the bosom of his Organisation. In truth, he needed all the help he could get.'

'And who better than his own flesh and blood,' I observed.

'In spending some time with her at Pelham House, it was quite clear to me that despite his rejection of her as a child, Cordelia had great admiration, loyalty to, and maybe even a twisted kind of affection for her father. She understood his motives in distancing himself from her.'

'Birds of a feather.'

'Indeed. When the Professor died, she became determined to resurrect his Organisation. It was a slow and careful procedure.'

Holmes paused and allowed himself a sardonic smile. 'When I made my return to life – if I may use such a dramatic phrase – Cordelia was determined to destroy me and gain revenge for her father's demise. She could, of course, have had me picked off by a sniper's bullet, but that would have been too easy for her. She wanted to taunt me, frustrate me, unnerve me and then issue the final blow herself. No doubt she was watching as the church fell around me.'

'And she nearly succeeded.'

'Ironically, my near-death experience in St Bartolph's gave me the opportunity to fight back.'

'And win the day.'

Holmes nodded sadly. 'Yes. However, I cannot help but feel a sense of guilt at her death. I should have prevented it.'

'I don't wish to be callous, Holmes, but if you had prevented it, you would only have saved her for the gallows. At least she died her own mistress.'

'I suppose you are right. That is the clear-headed objective view, of course.'

'They never did find the body though, did they?'

Holmes shook his head. 'Lestrade organised a search of the trackside either side of the areas where she leapt from the train but have found nothing. As a precaution I have my sources in France on the alert for any signs that she survived. However, no doubt she is lying concealed in some thicket somewhere, her corpse now the prey of all kinds of vermin.'

'That certainly is an unpleasant end, but it is an image you should not dwell on, my old friend.'

'I will try not to.'

'Just think of the success of this case and the praise given to you by the fellows at Scotland Yard. Even the Commissioner himself sent you a telegram. Most of the gang rounded up, all those ne'er-do-wells in the Dormitory arrested, as were all those on the list of the Organisation's associates – some of them quite high-ranking individuals – and Pelham House routed, all thanks to you.'

'Or rather Nigel Harrison.'

'Him, too.' We chuckled at this observation and then fell into silence as we circumnavigated the lake. After some time, Holmes asked, 'Are you hungry, Watson?'

'Now you come to mention it, I believe I am.'

'What say you to an early dinner at Marcini's?'

'That sounds like a capital idea.'

'Then it is settled. Marcini's it is. And perhaps I can practise some more of my Italian.'

'Oh, heaven forbid,' I said.

Holmes bellowed with laughter and we strode off briskly in the fading light.

About the Author

David Stuart Davies is one of Britain's leading Sherlockian writers. He was editor of *Sherlock Holmes – The Detective Magazine*, authored several Holmes novels, the hit play *Sherlock Holmes: The Last Act*, Titan's *Starring Sherlock Holmes* and a biography of Jeremy Brett. He is a member of The Detection Club and contributed commentaries to DVDs of the Basil Rathbone Holmes films and the Granada Brett series.

For more fantastic fiction, author events,
exclusive excerpts, competitions, limited editions and more

VISIT OUR WEBSITE
titanbooks.com

LIKE US ON FACEBOOK
facebook.com/titanbooks

FOLLOW US ON TWITTER AND INSTAGRAM
@TitanBooks

EMAIL US
readerfeedback@titanemail.com